THE FOSTERS
KEEP YOUR FRENEMIES CLOSE

THE FOSTERS
KEEP YOUR FRENEMIES CLOSE

Stacy Kravetz

Kingswell Teen
Los Angeles * New York

For information address Kingswell,
125 West End Avenue, New York, New York 10023.

Editorial Director: Wendy Lefkon
Executive Editor: Laura Hopper
Design: Arlene Schleifer Goldberg

ISBN 978-1-4847-1620-5
V475-2873-0-14346
Printed in the United States of America
First Paperback Edition, January 2015
10 9 8 7 6 5 4 3 2 1

SUSTAINABLE FORESTRY INITIATIVE
Certified Chain of Custody
Promoting Sustainable Forestry
www.sfiprogram.org
SFI-01054
The SFI label applies to the text stock

"I kept expecting someone to out me as the one person there who didn't measure up to expectations."

—Callie

THE FOSTERS
KEEP YOUR FRENEMIES CLOSE

Chapter 1

There's something strange about the clock above the door. Every time the second hand sweeps past the fat black number ten and makes its way to the eleven, the clock hums like it's digesting a swarm of bees. Then back to silence. Looking around the room, I expect everyone in the class to have the same interrupted train of thought I have when the humming kicks in every fifty-five seconds, but no one else seems to be bothered. They're just deep in thought. Or devoid of thought. Lucky either way.

I've never been a clock-watcher. Actually, that's not even close to being true. Especially in Ray's class, where it's almost impossible not to think about what's going to

1

happen in the hallway outside the classroom. I mean, it's inevitable, right? There's going to be drama, or at the very least, it's just going to be damned uncomfortable. Because that's how we left things, not really knowing where any of us stood.

I should back up. None of what's definitely about to get weird would have happened at all were it not for the past weekend. A weekend of bonding and twisted approximations of friendship. It started on Thursday.

We were here in this same classroom, only there was a distinct rumble of excitement because we were just one day away from the weekend. Everyone could feel it, the anticipation of something fun in the making; knowing that most of us would be at Kelsey's party and that the conversation Monday morning would probably involve something that went down there.

I looked over at Mat, who held his phone in his lap, texting someone without Ray noticing. His phone was buried under a blue sweatshirt, but I could see his right thumb tapping on the keyboard, while he held a pencil in his other hand, positioned over the paper on his desk, pretending to take notes.

The rest of us were copying down the outline on the board. It listed twelve American revolutionaries and their main contributions to the war. Ray always pulled test questions directly from his lectures and my social studies grades had not exactly been stellar lately. I needed all the help I could get. It's not that I didn't study. It's just that my studying was pretty ineffective.

"Next week's test is the last of the semester before finals," Ray said. The class let out a collective cheer of approval.

"Take this opportunity to study, people. Study tonight. Study this weekend. There's a lot to cover and cramming next week isn't going to cut it." A smattering of chatter broke out. No one really wanted to spend extra time studying for a test that wouldn't be on our radar for a week. I considered it for about four seconds and then put it out of my mind. Ray would organize study groups and have kids spend hours on optional material. Only the really type A kids took him up on them. That's not me.

But I didn't have time to hear about Ray's fabulous nerd idea because the intercom buzzed and interrupted his monologue. He answered, turning away from the class and speaking quietly into the mouthpiece, nodding, even though no one on the other end of the line could see him. I let my mind wander again to the clock, which continued its irritating tock, tock, tock. When Ray turned around to face us again, I snapped out of my lazy daze. He was looking right at me.

"Callie, you're needed in the assistant principal's office." That was strange. I'd never been called out of class to see Lena before. Couldn't this wait until I got home? Or at least later on, when I wasn't forced to endure the embarrassment of being dragged to detention or whatever else in front of the whole class? Weird. I gathered my papers up and shoved them into the pocket of my green folder. I crammed my American history book into my backpack along with the pink-and-orange scarf I'd been wearing all week, even though the weather had been pretty nice. It was a present from Lena and I knew it made her happy when she saw me wearing it. It would not be cool to lose it. Especially now.

"Callie," Lena said, full of bright energy, before I'd even set a foot past the threshold. I felt a dull lump of dread drop from my chest to my stomach. Lena's extra-bright smile wasn't helping matters. It was like she was overcompensating for whatever brand of awful she had in store for me.

"Everything okay?"

"Oh, of course, yes. I should've said that. Sorry."

"Feels so official, being called to the principal's office. But it's not really that. I mean, not when your foster mom is the vice principal. It's more just like going to visit someone at work. Informal. Right?"

Lena dug through the pile of papers on her desk and tried to avoid the question. "Well, it's a little more official than that. I mean, it's something I think we need to talk about here, instead of at home."

That lead anvil burrowed its way into my gut again. "What did I do?"

"Oh, sweetie, nothing. You didn't do anything. It's not like that."

"Well, what, then? Why the big emergency intervention? It's not, like, someone's birthday or something, is it? Did I miss a conversation?" I asked.

Lena's smile faded slightly, and I could tell she was making a great effort to keep looking cheerful while she wound up for the punch.

"No. Nothing like that. It's about your grades this semester." Of course it was. It didn't take a genius to see that I wasn't a genius. And months of missing school and spending time at Girls United hadn't done much for my grade point average. But I could work this out. That was why she'd called me in here, to tell me she understood. She knew how hard I'd tried. Or at least how I'd meant to try harder.

"I'll work harder, I swear. These next few months before the end of the year, I'll really kick it into gear." I hadn't sat down in the empty chair in front of Lena's desk, even though it had been pulled out at an inviting angle, suggesting I stay a while. I couldn't sit. It would be admitting I really deserved to be here, discussing my academic future with a school administrator. But this was just me having a casual conversation with my foster mom. Right?

"It's not really about that," Lena said. "I'm sure you'll

do the work you have in front of you. This project is about making up for what you missed."

"What project?"

"It'll be an independent study. The principal's approved it. And all you'll need to do is attend the weekend retreat and write a paper in order to make up for what you missed."

"Wait, wait. I'm going on a retreat? What even is that? It sounds like some kind of yoga cult thing."

"No, no. That's not what it is at all. It's just a weekend community service project with some other kids. You go, do good work for the world, and write about it. To be honest, I'm a bit envious."

"Right, yeah. The thing is, I'm not like a big tree hugger and I've already done my share of picking up garbage on the side of the freeway. This doesn't exactly scream my name." But based on the way she was looking at me, I got the feeling it had my name all over it.

Then I saw why. Lena pulled out a copy of my transcript and flipped it around to where I could see the list of marks I'd gotten all semester long. I was surprised to see that most of them were Cs and a few of the grades were missing entirely. I looked at her.

"Sweetie, this is your only option. Unless you want to repeat a grade, stay back next year." Lena would make an awesome lawyer. She negotiated like a pro. The only thing worse than the idea of *optional* mandatory work on a weekend was an entire repeat school year. I was in.

"Sounds like I don't have a choice," I said, noticing the relief flooding Lena's face when she saw I was getting her drift.

"Not really. The only choice is which project you'd like to take on. I've pulled together a few possibilities." She shuffled the papers on her desk again, pulling a stack of folders from under her calendar. Always organized and on point, Lena.

"Wow, you really gave this some thought," I said, feeling the heft of at least a dozen fat folders in my lap. The first one had a picture of a blue smiling whale on the cover in an ocean filled with bottles and garbage.

"I wanted you to have some options, so you could find something and really get into it."

I fanned through the folders, one "opportunity" worse than the next. "Do they honestly think anyone would be willing to spend a weekend shoveling out toilets?"

Lena looked sympathetic, but I immediately realized her sympathy didn't lie with me. "Imagine not having a toilet. This is life-improving work. It's not just about you."

"Clearly." But I knew she was right. I'd gotten myself into my share of messes, and it was up to me to dig my way out, one latrine at a time. It was not how I'd pictured spending an entire weekend, but then again, a lot of my life choices had landed me in worse places.

She tapped the folders. "I'm sure you can find something," she said, and I couldn't tell whether she'd already picked one of these "experiences" out for me in her mind. "There's one this weekend, if you just want to get it out of the way." That was one way of thinking about it.

"What is it?"

"I don't have all the information, but it definitely involves hard hats, rakes, dirt, and rocks. You'll be maintaining trails or creating new ones with the park service. It'll be an incredible project, actually. It's two days of volunteering on the statewide trails project. You take a bus to Vista, spend a night. Or two." She was doing her best to hold on to her smile, almost like she was compensating for me, urging me to take up the cause and smile, too.

"You have got to be kidding me." The words came out before I had time to think.

"Not kidding at all," Lena said. "It'll be good for you. The outdoors . . ."

I wasn't buying it.

"Is there—I don't know—maybe a different project we could do? One that doesn't involve, you know, dirt and rocks?" I asked.

Lena looked over her paperwork, though it was probably for show. She looked up like she'd read the tea leaves and learned my final destiny. "'Fraid not. At least, not this weekend. But I'm told it's a wonderful program.

8

The motto is 'Hard work, no pay, miserable conditions . . . and more!'" She was practically giddy, like she'd just sealed the deal with that ringing endorsement.

"So it's, like, settled? This is happening?" I asked.

Lena pulled together a neat little pile, Xerox copies of all the tests I'd barely passed and the missing assignments I'd somehow lost along the way. "You have a lot to make up for. And your community will thank you. So will your history grades."

I found the folder she was talking about. It was blue with a photo of a forest on the cover. "Sure, yeah."

Lena swiveled her chair around and pulled a fresh permission slip off her printer, then signed on the line where a parent okay was required. My fate was sealed.

"Okay . . ." I said. I pulled the scarf off and stuffed it into my bag. I suddenly felt uncomfortably hot.

"See you after school? I promised Stef I'd make that curry you all love." Lena already considered this issue closed.

"Sure. I'm studying with friends, but it won't be late."

I turned to leave, already dreading the longer conversation about grades and commitment I knew we'd be having later tonight. It was like Lena could read my thoughts.

"You need to do this. It's part of getting a fresh start around here." I didn't have to turn around to know her face held a look of concern.

I nodded and headed back to class.

Chapter 2

Mariana was already home in the kitchen when I walked in. "Hey. Anyone else home yet?" I asked her.

"Nope. Just me," she said without looking up, an expression of intense focus and a little bit of pain on her face. I looked at the array of snacks she had laid out on the countertop: a pile of sliced carrots, two bags of cheese puffs, and a container of crunchy kale chips Stef had gotten in the habit of baking for us.

"C'mon, just go for the real thing. Denial's not worth this kind of agony." I grabbed a handful of cheese puffs and goaded her to follow. Like some kind of puff pusher.

Now she looked up and smiled sadly. "I've been trying hard all week to eat healthy. And I haven't lost a pound."

"Why are you trying to lose weight? You look great."

"Oh, please. Someone called me 'bootylicious' at school. You really think that's a compliment?" Unconsciously, she ran a hand over the back of her leg.

"Depends who said it. If it was a guy, definitely meant as flattery." Although I had a feeling it wouldn't matter who said it. Mariana had been feeling self-conscious ever since Kaitlyn had made a comment about her "round" face, which was Kaitlyn-code for fat.

Mariana resolutely ripped open the other cheese puffs bag and scarfed down a handful. Then she picked up a carrot and took a bite, as if to counteract the fake orange powder.

"Aha, so it was a guy! Who?" Was it a good idea to dwell on this? I wasn't sure. But the words were out of my mouth before I could stop them.

Mariana shook her head. "No one. Really."

I grabbed a second handful of cheese puffs and felt the salt sizzle on my tongue when I chomped one. "Tell me!" I could tell she wanted to. She just needed a little encouragement.

Mariana grabbed another handful, looked at them, and put them down on the counter. She grabbed another carrot. For sure neither of us was going for the kale.

"Were you seriously thinking about eating the kale?" I couldn't help asking. "Or was that just for show?"

"What do you mean? It's good. You don't like it?"

Even the smell of it made my stomach turn. I pushed it further away but I still felt like I was inhaling green.

"Um, no. I'd rather eat dirt." Which was what the kale chips tasted like to me, so it was kind of a wash. "So tell me about the guy."

"Look, it's nothing. I'm not even sure he was talking about me. It's just something I overheard Chase say by the lockers." She looked away from me, pretending to pick something up off the floor. The subject of Chase was still a delicate one, and I knew that crush had died hard.

"Okay, so maybe it wasn't even about you. You definitely shouldn't get some big food complex over something that might have been about someone else." I took some more cheese puffs to emphasize my point.

"Well, he was looking right at me when he said it." Mariana blushed.

"I maintain my position. If he said it, it was a compliment. Seriously. Don't eat that crap just because of what someone might have meant when he said something that might have been about you."

Finally, Mariana smiled. "You're so right. I've been torturing myself, probably for nothing." But sorta enjoying it, I could tell. It gave her a reason to think about Chase all week, for one thing.

"Of course I'm right."

"But totally wrong about the kale. It's really good. And totes healthy."

"Totes?"

She shrugged.

"I don't notice you eating it," I pointed out.

Mariana shrugged and grabbed a fringy piece, popping it in her mouth to prove her point. Just the crunching made my skin crawl. "So why are you home early? I thought you were studying with friends."

"Yeah, I'm gonna do that later. Right now I gotta figure out my life a little bit."

"Wow, that sounds kinda drama queen," she said. "You could just say you have stuff to do."

Yep, I realized how it sounded. All this time I'd been holding my book bag on my shoulder like I was planning to bolt for the hills. I dropped it on the table and took my first deep breath since setting foot in Lena's office and learning about my fate for that weekend.

"I just found out I have to do this lame community service project to make up for all the school I missed when I was at Girls United." Saying it out loud made it sound a little better than I'd thought.

Mariana perked up at the idea—not the idea of community service, but the idea that we could talk about someone else's issues for a while instead of hers.

"Really? Like, mandatory beach cleanup or whatever?"

"Something like that." I still had the pile of folders stuffed in my book bag, though I'd actually thrown out a few of the really heinous-sounding ones, like being part of a musical that was going to be performed at an old-age home. Not that I don't see the value of entertaining people who probably don't get many visitors, but I am not a theater kind of person, and I was pretty sure that unleashing my singing voice on anyone would qualify as punishment, not entertainment. "I'm actually probably doing this thing where we plant trees and stuff for Earth Day."

"That doesn't sound so bad. Trees are cool."

"I know, right? I mean, how bad can it be?" I was trying to convince myself, not Mari.

She laughed. "I don't know."

I reached into my bag and pulled out the stack of folders. Maybe it was worth looking through them again. Just because Lena had suggested the weekend cleanup project didn't mean it was really the best one.

"Here are the choices." I fanned out the folders for Mariana to see. She read the stickers on the front covers: "San Diego Water Reclamation Project. Anchor Beach Sewage Project. Earth Day Forest Project. Tijuana Latrine Project. Children's Hospital Singing Project."

She looked up at me, pity in her eyes. "I'd stay away from anything with sewage or toilets, personally. But that's just me." For a moment, I wished I was her, worrying what a guy might think, mired in normal teenage problems. Instead, I always had what seemed like adult problems, or at least problems that were bigger than me.

"No, I hear you. Could these be worse? One choice

is more hideous than the next. That's why I was leaning toward the forest thing." I was doing my best to convince myself that I really was outdoorsy enough to handle it. My cell phone beeped with a text message: *What time are we studying?* I didn't answer right away. All I wanted to do was curl up on the floor and make this all go away. There had to be another way to get my grades up.

"You should see your face," Mariana said. "You look like you're being tortured. It's just carrying rocks around and building stuff. It seems like it could be cool to build a bridge or whatever." I nodded, trying to see it her way. Who was I kidding? It didn't sound cool at all.

"I guess it's not really supposed to be fun, right?" she said. "'Cause it's kind of a punishment." Why did I suddenly feel like stuffing the whole container of kale in my mouth? Like if I punished myself this way, maybe I could make the other punishment go away. Mariana sighed.

"You okay?" I asked.

"Yeah. I mean, maybe I could go with you. It's not like I have much going on this weekend, and at least I could get some extra credit or something." See, that's the difference between me and Mariana. She would do something like this voluntarily, just for the company and the chance to do something different. Why was I missing that gene? It really was time to stop feeling sorry for myself and get on board with this weekend.

Mariana started looking through the materials in the

forest project folder. For the first time, I really focused on what the weekend had in store for me. A group of teens. Kids I didn't know and who didn't know me. A fresh start with people who didn't have any idea of what I was about. Maybe that could be cool.

"Really, do you think Lena and Stef would let me go along?" Mari asked. "It's probably more fun than I'll be having if I stay here." I shrugged. The idea of having Mariana with me definitely made it sound more bearable.

"Would Lena and Stef let you do what?" came a voice from the next room. Lena poked her head through the doorway and came over to kiss Mariana on the cheek. "How was your day, sweetie?" She took stock of the snacks, popping a handful of kale chips into her mouth before spitting them out in a paper towel.

"Okay, these are awful."

"I'll make sure and tell Stef you said so. Am I really the only one who likes them?" Mariana asked with a smirk.

"Stef made these?" Lena asked with a sense of duty. She took one more chip and chewed it up and swallowed with some effort. Then she went to the fridge, took out an iced tea, and slugged down half the bottle. "They're kind of okay, once you get used to them, huh?"

"Whatever you say," I told her.

"So what's this you're planning to do that I need to approve of?" she asked Mariana, her eye going to the array of folders on the counter.

"Callie's weekend trip. I was thinking maybe I could—"

"Oh, no, you couldn't," Lena said, cutting her off. Mariana's face fell. I realized how her fluctuating social status lately had taken a toll on her. "I applaud your initiative, but this is Callie's to take on. Next year, when the opportunity comes for extra credit, you are more than welcome to choose one of the service learning projects, but not this time." I looked at Mariana and saw she was maybe more disappointed than I was.

Stef looked at her phone for the third time in an hour. "You told her to be home by nine, right?"

Lena nodded and took a sip of her wine. "I told her. And it's ten to nine, so she's not late. Don't worry."

Stef had been on edge since Lena told her about the community service project, and Lena had to admit her reasoning was valid, but she held her ground. This project would be good for me.

"I just wish you'd talked with me about this before arranging this whole thing," Stef said for the second time that night.

"I told you. It was a school decision. It's the only way to get her through to passing this year. Do you really want to see her held back a grade? My back was against the wall here." Lena picked up the remote to turn on the TV but hesitated, knowing Stef wasn't done with the conversation.

Stef kicked her shoes off and looked at the time again. "I'm just not thrilled about the idea of her going off with a bunch of kids on academic probation. They're not the kind of role models she needs right now."

"Wait, is that what you're worried about? 'Cause there's just as much chance that these kids are the opposite type, the ones looking for extra credit and stuff to put in their college essays. Those kinds of kids would be great for Callie to be around," Lena said.

Stef wasn't convinced. "But we don't know for sure, do we?"

"No, we don't know for sure. But this is one of those times when we just have to trust Callie to hold her own, no matter who she's around. Besides, maybe she'll make some new friends who don't have parole officers," Lena said, scooting over on the couch and curling up closer to Stef, who nodded and looked at her phone one more time. Then she put her arm around Lena.

In the next room, I stood where I'd been for the past five minutes, wondering if Lena and Stef had anything else to say about me. I knew the probation officer comment was a dig at my friends from Girls United, but until I heard it out loud, I hadn't realized how far Lena and Stef still had to go to forgive me completely for everything that had happened months earlier.

"Hey, guys," I said, walking into the room, where

Stef's eyes were glued to her phone. I saw Stef's shoulders fall in visible relief that I was home on time.

"Callie, hi," Stef said. "Lena was just telling me about your weekend plans. Sounds like a great opportunity."

I came further into the room and perched on the edge of the couch. "Yeah, I'm gonna give it my all. Hope for the best." Lena smiled at Stef. It was like I could read her mind, and I saw she was in my corner: *See? Stop underestimating her.*

Stef nodded. "You know what? I like your attitude." She got up and came over to me, and I reached up to give her a hug. "I'll be interested to hear how it goes," Stef said.

"Yeah." I nodded. "You and me both."

Chapter 3

Somehow I'd made it through the twenty-four hours leading up to my forced communion with trees. The parking lot was full of cars and I could see the bus idling by the bathrooms. Crews of kids playing soccer and lacrosse peppered the grass field, and a small group of kids my age stood near the bus with their parents, who were seeing them off with care packages and kisses like they'd be gone for a month.

I looked around to see if there were any other kids from Anchor Beach Charter but I didn't recognize anyone in the sea of faces. I did see some moms who looked like they'd dressed for a fashion shoot: head-to-toe designer clothes, spiky heels, and expensive bags. At a park. At five in the afternoon. I looked at Stef in her workout clothes, which I knew she'd worn all day even if she hadn't worked out, because it was her day off. I had to love her for that.

"Hey, look who came to see you off," Lena said, looking over my shoulder. Brandon, Mariana, Jesus, and Jude were walking toward us, Mariana leading the way. "Surprise!" she said.

"You came!" I said. I felt a wave of tears well up. I was more nervous about going away for the weekend than I'd realized, nervous about being away from everyone. My family. It felt good to call them that.

"You didn't think we were gonna let you go without saying good-bye," Mariana said.

"Well, I did think it was a little weird that no one was home this afternoon when we were leaving," I said. I'd looked in everyone's rooms to say good-bye, and Stef made excuses for everyone: Brandon had band practice, Mariana was with friends, Jude was doing some sort of project.

"All part of Mariana's plan," Brandon said. Without thinking, I threw my arms around his neck. When I let go, he looked at me sideways, trying to figure out what was up. I didn't exactly know myself.

I looked around at all the kids loading up and suddenly felt overwhelmed, even by the good intentions of my own family, who'd come to see me off. Lena and Stef must have sensed I needed some space, because they picked up my sleeping bag and duffel. "We'll take these to the bus."

"Hey, do you by any chance have some gum or anything in the car?" I asked Brandon, needing a little space and feeling the sudden impulse to burst into tears.

"Sure," he said, leading me toward his car. "Be right back," he told the others. The parking lot was full and the glare of the afternoon sun made it hard to see where he'd parked.

He started walking but I was lagging behind, moving at a snail's pace, not wanting to get to the car too quickly or to the bus that would take me away from everyone until Sunday. "You okay?" he asked, knowing I wasn't. I shook my head.

"I'm not sure I can do this."

"I know you're not exactly nature girl, but I'm sure they wouldn't make you do anything you can't handle." He wasn't understanding the issue.

"It's not that. It's . . . I'm not sure I can be away from . . . everyone. The last time I left, I ended up in juvie, if you recall," I said, reminding him of when I'd run off with Wyatt and intentionally stolen a sandwich so I'd have a place to spend the night—in jail. "I can't see my way to the other side of this weekend without it ending badly. I guess I kind of don't trust myself."

He nodded. I knew I didn't need to say more. He

understood. We'd always have that bond; whether it was a brother–sister understanding or something deeper, it didn't matter. He knew I needed someone I could rely on. "You can do this. Even if you don't know it, believe that I know it. Just trust yourself. You're gonna be fine." We'd started walking back toward the group. I felt the inevitability of it all and faced it like I was walking to my doom.

Stef rushed up. "There you are. Callie, they're getting ready to go. With six of us, that's about a minute per good-bye and you'll just barely make it," she said.

"Okay. Thanks."

I looked at Brandon pleadingly once more, willing him to get me out of this. "You're gonna be fine. Really. If you feel anything weird, just text me, k?" I nodded. He leaned in and whispered, "No jumping off the bus at a rest stop and running for the border. If you text me to pick you up in TJ, I'm not coming."

I looked around to see if anyone else was torn up by a forced good-bye. Maybe there'd be a comrade-in-arms I could commiserate with. I saw one girl rocking a slouchy tie-dye peace bag over her shoulder, arm in arm with a guy on his way to the bus. Then they both got on. I saw another couple making out behind the bus. But after a few minutes of that hot and heavy session, they turned and walked deeper into the park, not even part of our weekend group. But no one seemed to be having trouble separating from family. I guess that's something most people get over when they're like ten years old.

The crowd had thinned and most of the kids had been swallowed up by the idling air-conditioned tourism bus, its tinted windows obscuring the faces inside. Most of the people standing around now were parents and even they were starting to head for their cars. I looked at Brandon again, my every fiber aching over having to do this. I knew I was feeling sorry for myself, but who could blame me? When faced with having to leave for two days and spend time shoveling dirt, wouldn't anyone be holding a personal pity party?

Stef and Lena wandered over, Lena tilting her head toward the bus. "Think you'd better get going. Last thing you want is to have us drive you out there."

"Last thing I want or last thing you want?" I asked. Lena gave me a hug and Stef leaned in and kissed my cheek.

"Have fun," Lena said. "Believe it or not, this can actually be a worthwhile experience. You may like it so much you'll be asking to go on another one." Her optimism wasn't as contagious as she may have hoped.

"Let's not push our luck," I said.

"I'll try to talk some sense into her," Stef said, leading Lena away from us but not daring to leave until they knew I was firmly situated on the bus. I guess trust would be a bit longer in coming. They both waved and I blew them a kiss. I leaned down and wrapped my arms around Jude, looking away so he wouldn't see the tears welling in my eyes. He hugged me back hard, almost too hard, and I knew he was worried that if he let me out of his sight, I might not come back. "I'll see you in forty-eight hours. Promise," I told him. He nodded and hugged me once more. I couldn't believe how tall he'd gotten and I chose to focus on that rather than the fact that I wouldn't see him for two days. Jude solemnly walked over to Lena and Stef, acting stronger than I felt.

I looked once more at Brandon, hating this good-bye more than usual. He'd managed to walk me all the way to the door of the bus without me even realizing I was about to be released for boarding.

"One final reminder, everyone," yelled a tall, broad-shouldered African American woman next to the bus. "No cell phones or electronics of any kind. This weekend we're all gonna unplug."

I turned to Brandon with panic in my eyes. How was I going to text him if I couldn't have anything electronic? If I'd been feeling anxious before, the panic ratcheted up a million degrees at the thought of a weekend without a cell phone. I made a snap decision to keep my phone hidden and sneak out when I wanted to text him. But then I turned and saw Lena with her hand outstretched. She wasn't about to let me break the rules.

Brandon nodded at me encouragingly, willing me to

believe everything would be okay, but I couldn't stem the panic. "Meet me tomorrow night. I'll sneak out." He looked alarmed at the thought. "It'll give me something to look forward to and I'll be able to relax until then." I didn't even know how I was gonna do it, but there had to be a way. I'd deal with that one once I got there. I stepped onto the bus, imploring him with my eyes to say yes. "C'mon," I mouthed to him. Stef and Lena were watching us. He looked panicked.

"You'll get thrown off the trip."

"No, I'll be super careful, I swear. Just meet me. I'll start walking south outside the gate and you meet me on the road. At like eight-thirty, once it's good and dark."

"Okay, okay, sure," he said. "Now go and have fun." He stepped away to stand with Lena and Stef. I had no choice but to get on the bus now and face whatever this weekend held in store.

There was a seat toward the front. Two, actually, which suited me fine, because I wasn't looking for someone who'd want to talk the entire ride to the forest site.

I leaned my forehead against the glass, trying to decipher what Brandon was saying to Lena. I couldn't read any of it, but Lena laughed and the three of them started walking back toward the parked cars.

So intently was I focused on the activity outside that I didn't even notice someone had come and sat down in the empty seat next to me. That is, until she said my name.

"Hey, Callie. I didn't know you were on this trip." I turned to see who could possibly already know my name. And wouldn't you know, it was Talya.

Chapter 4

"So . . . here we are," I said. Stating the obvious. I looked around to see if there were any other empty seats on the bus. Most were taken, but I saw a few empties and I considered bolting for the safety of someone who didn't know me. I mean, Talya and I had made our peace, I guess, but there would always be something uncomfortable between the two of us.

She was sitting in the outer seat, though, so moving would require an awkward hop over her, and I couldn't come up with a reasonable excuse for needing to switch. So I was stuck. For a three-hour bus ride to the mountains. I just hoped Talya wouldn't puke in my lap when we hit the winding part.

"Yeah, here we are. Lucky us. Maybe we'll be room-mates," she said sarcastically. I looked around again and noticed the empty seats had actually been claimed by kids who'd been hovering in the aisle, so maybe Talya had no choice but to sit next to me. And she was no more thrilled about it than I was. I could tell.

"So. Like three hours, huh?" I said. "Long time on a freezing cold bus."

"Well, you can turn the air down," she said, reaching up to adjust the fan blowing on me from above. "Actually, it's broken."

"Awesome."

"We could switch. Seats, I mean. If it's really bothering you," she said. I didn't want her doing me any favors, and besides, I'd gotten all my stuff stowed under the seat. But Talya had already gathered her stuff in her lap and stood up next to me, waiting for me to scoot to the aisle. "This is bet-ter, right?" she asked as I rearranged myself in the new seat.

"Yeah. Thanks." Now I kind of owed her and we'd barely been gone ten minutes. So awkward. I reached into my bag and fished around for something to do, a book to read, anything. But I'd only packed a few snacks and a pair of sunglasses. I pulled out an old crappy MP3 player and unraveled the headphones, finding salvation in a little Bruno Mars to tune all this out. But no sooner had I put the headphones on than one of the trip leaders was right in my grill, shaking her head.

"Sorry. I'm gonna have to keep those for you till Sunday." She turned to the group and announced, "We're promoting unity on this trip and that requires everyone get to know each other and work together. The paperwork you signed acknowledges you understood the rules. You'll have access to a phone in the office if there's an emergency." I hadn't even looked at the paperwork before signing it. I looked at the trip leader, the same pretty black woman who'd herded us onto the bus earlier and delivered the no-cell-phone edict. She looked to be in her twenties, with long cornrows and a Grateful Dead shirt. If she hadn't been reprimanding me, I'd think maybe she was cool. Instead I kind of growled and handed over the tiny MP3 player.

"There. Done, okay?"

"Thanks. What's your name?" she asked.

"Callie."

"Hi, Callie. Jamie. Glad to have you on board." She smiled and returned to her seat at the front of the bus. I just hoped she didn't plan to lead us in song. That would seriously put me over.

"Guess they really mean business about the whole serving-the-community thing," Talya said. She unwrapped a protein bar and read all the ingredients on the wrapper before taking a bite. I could hear her jaw cracking when she chewed.

"Yeah."

"I can't afford to screw this up. My grade depends on it." She looked vulnerable. Like she might break in two. I guess it was a pretty honest thing to say. She was trying to make this work, the two of us here.

"I'm in the same boat. I missed a lot of school, you know, when I was away." If she could admit her weakness, I figured I could meet her halfway. "Apparently this weekend will tip the balance toward me actually passing this year."

Talya looked confused. "Wait, you mean this is mandatory for you?"

Now it was my turn to be mystified. "Well, yeah. Isn't that what you were saying?"

"Oh. No," she said, looking embarrassed. Or proud. I couldn't tell. "I'm doing it for extra credit. Just to cement my A in Ray's class."

"Right. Sure. Cement your A. Makes sense." I rolled my eyes. Those were not words that would ever come out of my mouth.

She looked out the window and didn't talk for a while. I debated putting my hoodie up and burying my nose in a magazine to tune her out. But before I could, Talya looked back at me. "I'm not the enemy, you know."

"What's that supposed to mean?"

"Just that whatever your deal is, with Brandon or with some kinda baggage from being in juvie, that's not on me. I'm just trying to get by."

KEEP YOUR FRENEMIES CLOSE

I was about to ask what the hell she meant by that when the streaked-blond nest of hair in front of us whipped around, revealing plump pink lips and massive designer sunglasses. "Wait, you're that girl? The one who was, like, in jail? I heard about you. We all did," she said, gesturing around to no one in particular.

"Awesome," I said. "What, did they like put out a bulletin before the trip: beware of the ex-con?"

The blonde laughed. "No. I didn't mean that. I meant I heard about you from my friend at ABCC. Kelsey?" She smiled like she expected me to join in the love-fest for Kelsey, which was kinda hard to do, given what she'd put Mariana through.

"How do you know Kelsey?" I was already setting myself up to avoid the blond bomb for the rest of the weekend. Not to judge, but if she was good friends with Kelsey, she might be just like her.

"Oh, from like forever ago. I actually went to Anchor Beach for a year. We're not super close anymore, but I saw her at a party and she gave me all the dirt on the kids at school. She said you were new." She left it hanging there like I was supposed to fill in the blanks, which I had no desire to do. "I'm Gracie, by the way. Up there's Riley." She pointed at the girl who'd been sitting in the seat next to her but who now held court in the aisle of the bus, talking to a couple of guys two rows up. Riley turned and waved when she heard her name but she didn't seem particularly interested in Gracie's sudden desire to talk to me. She kept running a finger down a strand of hair that had come loose from a tiny clip holding back her long brown curls and flipping it out of her face. She was one of those girls with a slight build and bouncy breasts who didn't seem to know how good she had it. Riley was wearing a white tank top and her gray bra strap hung down over her tanned arm. She either didn't notice it or didn't care. I could see the outline of her thong underwear through her gray sweatpants, which hung on her tiny frame.

"People, I need you in your seats." Jamie reprimanded us from the front of the bus, eying Riley, who hadn't moved the past two times Jamie had said it. "That means you, Riley." Riley made a pouty face and scooted back into the seat next to Gracie.

"Hey," she said to Talya and me. For a minute, I'd forgotten Talya was even there. Gracie hadn't acknowledged her and she had her head tucked into a book. "I'm Riley."

"I already told Callie that," Gracie said.

"Well, how's I supposed to know? Okay, so who's your roommate?" she asked, pointing to Talya. I felt suddenly ill. Just because we were sitting next to each other on the bus didn't mean Talya and I would be roommates. Did it? Talya picked her head up from her book and smiled at Gracie and Riley and, shock of shocks, the three of them started chatting nonstop like they'd been friends for years.

"Oh my god, I know her. That's the one with the pink ombré hair. I think at this point she's doing it as a statement because that fad ended long ago," Gracie said, referring to someone I didn't know. Talya laughed. "She's an outlier. She didn't even do the pink until after everyone else stopped doing it. Callie, you would like her," she said.

"Who?" I asked, not really sure I cared.

"Morgan Shelley. She goes to their school," Talya said. "I've been friends with her forever. Our parents were friends before we were born and she's practically family."

"Isn't it such a small world?" Riley squealed. "Morgan was going to come on this trip but her parents whisked her off on some kind of family reunion trip. She'll be so bummed she missed all the fun." I perked up at the word *fun*. Maybe there was something I'd missed in the description of the weekend, but if these girls who looked like partiers were thinking this was going to be a good time, maybe I'd underestimated the potential.

"So where do you guys go to school?" I asked.

"Anchor Prep," Riley said like it was obvious. "This is going to be such a party. Jaden and Max'll DJ tonight and I think they brought some vodka. But even if not, I heard we can sneak some alcohol from the guy who runs the kitchen. Supposedly he's a lush and he keeps a supply in

a locked cabinet. You brought your crowbar, right, Max?"
she said, tapping the guy in the seat ahead of her. He
turned and flashed a Cheshire cat grin. He nodded at me.
"'Sup?" Before I could answer, he'd turned back around
and was high-fiving the guy next to him, who'd just
slammed an iced cappuccino. I assumed he was Jaden.
He had light brown hair, which he kept running his hand
through unconsciously before slapping a Cubs baseball
cap on and turning it backward.

"Yo," he said, acknowledging Talya and me.

"Hey!" Talya said. "Count me in for sure. I'm always up
for a party." She nudged me in the ribs. I knew I needed
to stay above the fray and avoid doing anything that
might get my school prison sentence extended. Stealing
booze and sneaking around probably didn't qualify as
model behavior. I nodded weakly and pretended to fish
something out of my bag.

"Yo. I was talking to you." I looked up and saw that
Jaden had hopped out of his seat and was now hovering over me, looking into my bag as I rifled through. I
dropped it on the floor of the bus and met his gaze.

"Yeah?" I said.

"You up for a party?" He draped his body over the
bench seat in front of me and popped his cap up, ran
a hand through his hair, and put it back on. His bicep
flexed when he did it.

"Sure. Maybe." I pasted on a forced smile.

36

"Dude, what's up with your tight friend?" he said to Talya.

"Oh, don't worry, Callie's cool. She'll be there." She looked at me with an insistent expression: *Don't ruin this for me.*

I nodded, just wanting this conversation to end. Jaden kept his gaze focused on me for a minute. He was the kind of guy who knew he was hot and was just waiting for me to acknowledge it, which I didn't. He waited a minute longer, focusing on me, trying to figure me out. Then he nodded, too, and went back to his seat.

"So, Riley, how'd you get roped into doing community service?" I asked, desperate to get on to a new topic.

"Oh, that? My parents are paying me to do it. I need it for my college apps and my parents get that it's cheaper to give me a few hundred bucks to do this than to send me to some African refugee camp to shoot a video on poverty."

I hoped the shock didn't register on my face. "Some kids do that?"

She looked at me like I'd just grown an extra set of eyes. "Sure. I mean, of course. Some parents'll do anything to get their kids into a good college." If I didn't feel like an alien before, I'd now left planet Earth and was orbiting some faraway place.

Chapter 5

The camp was nothing like I expected. I guess I'd prepared for the worst, imagining army barracks and a drill sergeant barking at us to swab the decks. Mixing metaphors here, I know. Jamie stood in front of the two dozen of us, giving a presentation on the forest service and the kind of work it did. She'd changed out of her Grateful Dead shirt and now wore a wide straw hat, a drab green pair of shorts, and a long-sleeved white shirt with an insignia on the front, like a park ranger uniform mixed with pajamas. It made her look a little older, a little more official, and kind of rumpled at the same time.

We sat under a tan tarp on two wooden picnic benches. The area was surrounded by tall pine trees whose fallen needles made a squishy carpet under my feet. Behind Jamie stood the one-story building where we'd dumped our stuff in an office after the bus ride. I wouldn't exactly call it nice, but let's face it: after being in juvie, it didn't take much for a place to look like paradise. I hadn't seen any bedrooms in the building, but from the look of the office, I'd rate it somewhere in the neighborhood of a roadside motel. I'd seen worse.

"We've got big work ahead of us, people," Jamie was saying when I shook the cobwebs from my brain and started paying attention. "Trees to be planted, rocks to be hauled. I hope you didn't bring outfits to go clubbing and whatnot. You're gonna get real familiar with dirt and splinters. And if you're lucky, we'll take a special field trip to the garbage dump and haul out some trash."

Gracie and Riley were looking around the group, like they were trying to figure out which unlucky souls would be doing the dirty work because they sure as hell didn't plan to be hauling garbage. A squirrel ran down the trunk of a tree and froze, like it hadn't expected an audience.

Jamie pointed down a pathway through the trees. "You can kind of see them from here, those tentlike things? Those are your lofty accommodations, so you can get accustomed to dirt right off the bat." I guessed we wouldn't be staying anywhere near the nice-ish white building where we'd dropped our stuff. I tried to see some evidence of the tents but they were obscured by the branches of a tree in front of me.

Gracie whispered to Riley loud enough for me to overhear. "I heard you need to bring your own rug and air mattress to survive this place. Check!" I had been told no such thing, and I had a feeling that if any of that intel had been available, Lena would have kept it from me just for the sake of making this an "experience."

"So let's get to the good stuff: roommates, kitchen duty, and all." She took a page from behind the stack on her clipboard.

"Ugh, they didn't tell us there was gonna be KP," I heard Jaden say. I looked at him sympathetically. Fortunately, I'd more than covered the intricacies of KP at Girls United, so the thought of scrubbing a pot or two didn't throw me. I was more worried about the roommate situation.

"In tent two: Gracie, Talya, Callie, and Riley. Tent three: Max, Jaden, Sam, and Luke." She continued reading from her list of names. I wondered if it was a coincidence that the four of us had ended up on the bus near each other, kind of a preview of the get-to-know-yous that would come later. Of course it was intentional. Intended as torture.

Gracie turned and put her hand up for a high five. Talya slapped her hand. "Hey, so that means we're right near the boys' tent. Tent three," she whispered to me. I nodded, stood up like a robot about to walk the plank, and followed Jamie into the white building, where we retrieved our stuff and started down the path that led to our tents.

Number two was across the path from number four but I didn't see any sign of the tents where the guys were staying. "Odd numbers are on the other side of the river," Jamie said. "We're not dumb, y'all. It's not like we're gonna put boys and girls right next to each other. Besides, in the middle of the night, when you gotta jump out of your tent to pee, you don't want an audience."

Okay, that did it. "Wait, you mean there aren't bathrooms?" I asked. School credit or not, that just might be a deal breaker.

"Oh, we've got latrines up near camp. You can wash up and all there but I'm just saying, in the middle of the night, you probably don't want to hike up the road. Nature calls and you gotta give back to nature." I took a hard look at Jamie. She seemed pretty confident and even normal, but she was talking about peeing in the great outdoors like it was something we did every day. I looked at the rest of the group to affirm they felt the same way I did, but most of them weren't even paying attention. Talya was already sidling up to Jaden and talking him up about sports. "I heard you're a lacrosse star," she said.

"Oh, yeah? Where'd you hear that?"

"Gracie says you play."

"Yeah, I'm on the squad. Missing three workouts for this project. Better be worth it." He kicked at the dirt and a little cloud swelled up and covered his shoes in grime.

Talya pulled her hair out of her ponytail and let it fall over her shoulders. "You're not gonna get out of shape in one weekend, I'm sure," Talya said, looking him over. "You look pretty fit."

He smiled, clearly into having an admirer. "True. Not out of shape, but I need to be in peak form next week for a match."

"Well, maybe we can work out together here," she said suggestively, taking a step closer to him.

"Maybe we can."

Jamie, always there to bring us back to reality, stepped in and herded the boys down the road toward their own tents. "C'mon guys, time to check out your high-rent digs."

The guys grumbled at the intrusion and started ambling down the road after her. Except for one guy, who hung behind, watching us separate and lug our stuff into the tents. I looked up and he was smiling at me. And he was gorgeous. Not that I was looking, of course, but you kinda couldn't help noticing him. He had lazy green eyes under long lashes, which he blinked slowly, like he'd just woken up from a really great nap. Dark hair fell over his forehead and dropped over one eye. I looked away and hoisted my bag over my shoulder.

Gracie fell into step with me and whispered, "That's Austin. Babe, right?"

"I mean, I guess. He go to your school?" I turned to look back in his direction and saw that he was still standing there grinning at me.

"Nah, he doesn't go to Prep. He's at the academy down the coast. But he comes to all the parties. He's got this sweet ride, an old beemer from like the nineties that he had repainted neon green."

"Why's he waiting around?" I asked. I didn't dare look back again. Gracie took care of that for me.

"Oh, good. He bailed finally. I mean he's supremely hot, but let's just say he's not the kinda guy you want to bring home to meet your dad."

"What's that mean?"

"Just . . . trouble. In a good way. But trouble." Gracie hefted a big brown bag into the crook of her arm and walked toward our tent. "Am I gonna have to fight you for him?" she asked, laughing. I could tell she was only partly kidding.

"I, um . . . I'm not really looking," I said, maybe a little too quickly.

"Ooh, I'm sensing a story."

"No, nothing to tell, really. It's just, I mean—"

"Chill. I was just giving you a hard time. Whatever you've got going's cool. And I'm not even sure I'm into him. But I might get bored, so you never know," she said, staring at the tent like it was Everest. "C'mon. Let's see what we've gotten ourselves into."

We walked over to tent two. To call it a tent was to use the term loosely. There was no floor, just a four-sided wooden frame dug into the ground with a giant dirty tarp arranged over the top in the shape of a triangle. So it looked like a tent from far away and it was almost like a little room, save for the bare dirt floor and the huge gaps where the tarp didn't quite meet up with the frame on the sides. In other words, it would be freezing cold at night. There were actual beds, metal-framed bunks with thin worn mattresses. Four bunk beds per tent, so we each got our own and I wasn't forced to choose a top bunk and risk rolling off in the middle of the night.

"Okay, I seriously can't deal," Gracie said.

"Oh, quit being such a wuss," Riley said, taking Gracie's hand and leading her in. "Come appreciate the full splendor of our rustic scene." Gracie didn't look at all convinced by her optimism.

"Okay, whatever. Let's get a sheet on these before we spend too much time looking at them," Gracie said, unzipping her bag. She unfurled a flannel floral sheet and hurriedly draped it over a bottom mattress.

"I guess I'll take this one," I said, opening my bag to pull out a plain gray sheet and throwing it over my own bottom bunk.

"So this is the closet, I guess," Talya said, gesturing

to a row of nails pounded into the wooden frame to act as clothing hooks. "I guess they don't want us to get too comfortable."

"My essay is gonna include all of this," Gracie said, pulling out a bottle of room spray and spritzing the entirety of the place. "I bought this in Paris last summer."

"Good call," Riley said, whipping out a cashmere blanket and spreading it on the floor of the tent.

"Aren't you worried about that getting filthy?" Talya asked.

"I'll just dry-clean it. It's old anyway," she said.

I looked into my bag, willing some fabulous decorative item to appear where I knew there was nothing. "I didn't bring anything to make this place look any better," I said. "I didn't know."

"It's cool," Gracie said. "You help me if I decide I do want Austin and we'll call it even." I nodded, completely unsure how I was going to do that.

Chapter 6

Dinner that night was spaghetti in a trough and garlic bread so drenched in buttery garlic I was sure you could smell it for miles. Maybe it was a ploy to keep people from making out after dinner. I took two pieces, since there was no shot at that happening anyway. I grabbed a handful of baby carrots and munched on one while I took an empty spot on the picnic bench next to Jamie. "Hey."

"Hey. There's chocolate cake for dessert. So eat up," she said, twirling a forkful of spaghetti and popping it in her mouth like it didn't matter how it tasted.

"You a big spaghetti fan?"

"Food is food. We're lucky to have it," she said. "One

of the bonuses of spending time working outdoors is everything tastes better."

"Or in other words, if you're desperate, anything qualifies as fine dining?" I still wasn't convinced by her seemingly eternal optimism.

"More like you just appreciate everything a little bit more," she said quietly, looking me over. She was probably trying to make sense of what kind of person I was, along for the ride on this trip but ill-equipped to handle the outdoors. I noticed a folder stuffed with papers sitting in front of her.

"What's all that?" I asked.

"Medical releases, student data, forestry service info, pretty much my bible out here." She scooped up the pool of sauce on her plate with a piece of garlic bread and slugged down water from a metal canteen. "So, Callie, not that I don't appreciate the company, but why aren't you sitting with your friends?"

I looked around and saw Gracie holding court with Riley and two other girls who I knew were in tent four. Talya was glued to Jaden's side, laughing and twirling her hair and hanging on his every word.

"They're not really my friends. Not yet, anyway. So if you're cool with it, I'm good here."

She looked at them, too, but seemed to see them differently. "They look like a good group. Hard workers, here for a challenge." She patted her pile of papers and

I got the impression she knew things about all of us I'd never find out. I tried to imagine what information she might have on each of them.

"I'm cool with you hanging with me. But you know part of the weekend here is the bonding experience, so I'm gonna push you out of your comfort zone eventually. Consider yourself warned."

"Got it," I said. "Warned." I scooped up some spaghetti, which wasn't half bad. "Do you, like, live here?" I couldn't figure her out. She was so mellow about the whole rustic thing, and while there was a part of me that wanted to run for the hills, there was also a part of me that wanted to be more like her.

"Not full-time. But I do try to get out here whenever I can. It's just better living in nature, don't you think?" I nodded obediently. My look must not have been convincing. "You'll get there. Maybe not in one weekend, but you'll get a whole lot closer. So you've got that to look forward to."

"Sure, yeah."

Jamie stood up and brushed the garlic bread crumbs off her pants. "Now's where I push you out of the nest. Go sit with those guys over there." She pointed at an empty spot on the bench next to Max. He looked harmless enough, so I went over and plunked down next to him.

"Hey, you stole my spot," came a voice off to my right.

I looked up and saw Austin grinning down at me with

that same sleepy look. I don't know why, but he made me nervous.

"You were never sitting here," Max said.

"I know. I'm just giving her a hard time. Callie, right? That's your name?" He smiled at me again. He had a calm, easygoing way about him, a natural charmer.

"That's me."

"Cool. Just making sure I got that right." Max had leaned over to listen to a joke one of the other guys was telling, leaving Austin with his eyes locked on mine. I tried to figure out what it was about him that made my heart beat uncomfortably fast. I reminded myself that the last thing I needed on this weekend trip was a romantic complication. Not like I needed reminding. I wasn't interested in Austin but I couldn't quell the rush I felt when he came closer to me. It was matter over mind.

He leaned in and pulled something small out of his pocket and gestured for me to take a look: a vapor pipe. "You into it? It's strawberry-flavored, but I've got cinnamon and chocolate. Pick your pleasure. Later on, I'll come find you." He leaned in a little closer, like he knew the effect he could have on a person. "Check it," he said, and moved past me. I couldn't help looking him over as he swaggered over to the other table, slow like honey rolling off a spoon.

Even without reading the trip guidelines, I knew enough to imagine that smoking, vapor or otherwise, would get us kicked off the trip. I couldn't afford that even if I was into strawberry vapor, which I definitely wasn't. I noticed that Talya was sitting by herself, leaning against the tree where Jaden had been with her a few minutes ago. He was shoveling down a second piece of chocolate cake and laughing with Patrick, a guy from his tent. Talya watched him and didn't flinch when Austin sat down next to her. But she must have felt the same pull I did, because a moment later he had her full attention.

I couldn't hear what they were saying, but every time Austin spoke, Talya laughed and flirted like Jaden was a thing of the remote past. I watched as Austin playfully punched her in the arm and put a hand on her knee. Sure enough, a few minutes later, he showed her the pipe and I saw her nod. Of course she'd be into that. Whichever way the wind blew, Talya seemed game. She was different from the girl I knew from school. Maybe we were all trying out different versions of ourselves on this trip. I didn't know why I suddenly felt annoyed. It's not like I wanted Austin for myself, but a tiny part of me didn't like how quickly he'd moved on from me to Talya.

"Quite a sideshow, huh?" Max said. His friends had gotten up and now it was just the two of us on the bench. He was watching them, too. "That guy's bad news."

"Oh? Do you know him?"

"I know of him," he said, but didn't elaborate.

Max picked at the remains of his chocolate cake, which he'd cut into small squares and eaten only a few bites of. "If I was studying psychology, I could have a field day with that," I said, pointing to the cake.

"Yes, I flunked geometry and I have issues with my mother," he said, grinning. "Or I was bored."

"One or the other. Clearly."

The other guys had moved off and were throwing around a football on a square of dirt with a volleyball net. Neither of us said anything.

"Uncomfortable silence," Max said finally.

"And does calling it uncomfortable make it less uncomfortable?"

"No, but maybe talking does. See? Now no more silence."

I decided I liked Max. And liking one person on this trip just might be enough. He was easy to talk to and he didn't seem fixated on my status as the girl on the trip with her own personal parole officer.

A bird flitted down and stood at Max's feet, looking from one of us to the other, maybe figuring out the odds of scoring a crumb from either of us. "So are you here to score kiss-ass points for your college apps like, apparently, everyone but me?" I asked.

"Nah, I had mono earlier this year and missed a bunch of school. This is kinda just makeup work for me," he said, tossing a tiny crumb of cake to the bird. "So I take it you're not here to dazzle the admissions directors, either?"

I immediately regretted asking, because now I had to

return the favor and answer his question. But I shrugged and figured maybe he'd just let it go.

We watched Jamie sitting with a group of guys dealing cards in what looked like a poker game using pine needles as chips. She laughed at something one of them said and pounded the table with her fist, sending the needles flying. Max and I just sat in silence, but it didn't feel awkward anymore. After a few minutes, he spoke, looking straight ahead and talking in a quiet, even voice.

"I didn't really have mono. That's just what we told the school. And my friends." He took a deep breath, like he was preparing me for some big secret. Or preparing himself.

"Hey, sometimes you need to take the path of least resistance. Or just make it easy for other people to understand," I said, hoping it sounded reassuring.

"It was really more exhaustion, at least that's what my parents call it. But that's just because my mom is a tabloid junkie and she reads about celebs being hospitalized for exhaustion all the time. And it sounds better than saying your son basically snapped, went 'round the bend, which is about what happened."

I didn't know what to say. I just nodded and watched Max's expression, which stayed stoic but not uncomfortable. "Should I not have told you that?" he asked.

"Oh, no, I'm glad you told me. Makes me feel like I'm not the only one here who isn't on the path to Ivy greatness, for one thing. Plus, it's good to get stuff out." I was one to talk. Sometimes even if I wanted to talk about something, I just couldn't. "So you're doing better?"

"You could say. I mean, I'm not shutting myself in my room for days at a time and sobbing. Or lashing out at people, which is what was happening before." I couldn't believe he was telling me all this. Maybe he hadn't told anyone. But I still didn't understand, not really.

"What . . . happened?" I asked. Max shook his head and looked up at the trees. The bird had flown up to a branch and was watching his plate of cake, plotting its next move.

"It sounds so minor now. But at the time . . . I just . . . couldn't cope, you know?" I wasn't sure. I kind of felt like I did know. But everyone has trouble coping sometimes. Was he talking about something in particular? "It was just a bunch of things that all came together at once. My dad . . . he's a drinker, and a couple months ago we found out he'd lost, like, a whole bunch of other people's money and might be going to jail for it. And then my sister, she got checked into the hospital because she weighed like eighty-five pounds and had basically stopped eating, and I was supposed to be checking out colleges for lacrosse, only with the time I took off, now I'm probably going to have to wait a year. If the scouts are still interested in me at all." He exhaled a big breath. It was a lot of information and I was trying to digest it all.

"That's crazy intense," was all I could think to say. *Rich kids don't necessarily have it better,* I realized. Then I mentally reprimanded myself for being so dumb as to need a reminder. I mean, look at Sophia and everything she went through.

"You think?" He kind of laughed. "When I say it out loud, it almost sounds . . . I don't know. . . ."

"Yeah, that's how I feel sometimes when I talk about my life. And then I feel like a whiner for talking about it at all."

"Well, you'll have to tell me."

"I don't really do that. Tell people stuff."

"C'mon. I showed you mine. . . ." He was so honest and friendly it was easy to feel comfortable. So I opened up. A little. It felt strange, telling stuff to someone I barely knew. But easy and kind of a relief at the same time.

He just listened. Somehow I ended up unloading more than I planned, because he just kept nodding like it was all okay. I told him things about Jude and how I always worried more about him than I did about myself, some vague stuff about relationships and why I was definitely not looking to hook up that weekend. He didn't say anything. He didn't need to. I didn't talk about Liam. Or my biological father. Or Brandon. Some things don't need to be shared. But I told him a lot, more than I'd shared with pretty much anyone. I don't trust people, but for some reason I trusted him.

Chapter 7

The scene in front of the small bathroom mirror was nothing short of comical. We'd been told to be in our bunks by 10:00 with an absolute lights-out at 10:30, and at 9:55, you'd think we were putting on last-minute touches before going onstage, rather than brushing our teeth and getting ready for bed. Talya and Gracie were jockeying for prime position and applying eye makeup, and a girl named Kellan was shaking her long strawberry bangs into her eyes and flipping them away over and over again until she got the right combination of air and movement before spritzing them into submission with hairspray. Apparently no one was actually planning on going to sleep.

Let me just back up a moment and explain that the mirror wasn't even really a mirror. It was a small rectangle of metal that reflected enough to allow us to see ourselves, but it was hardly fit for runway prep. We were in the communal bathroom, which had dirty wood planks for a floor and dim lighting from a bare bulb hanging from the ceiling. A couple of bathroom stalls and two showers all in tight quarters made it feel uncomfortably cozy. But we made it work.

"I saw Jamie and Bryce go up the road to headquarters about fifteen minutes ago, so let's give it like another twenty and then we're probably safe," Kellan was telling Rachel, one of her roommates, who also went to Anchor Prep.

"I think Bryce's hot," Rachel said. "I'd follow him down a dark alley, no problem." Bryce was the other trip leader—Jamie's lesser half, as she'd called him. He'd smiled and said he couldn't exactly disagree. "Jamie's a beast on the trails," he told all of us.

"You think he and Jamie are, like, a thing?" Kellan asked, taking one more swipe at her mascara.

Gracie packed up her toiletries and headed for the door. "Nah," she said. "I'm guessing Jamie doesn't go that way. Just a feeling."

"Really? You think she's gay?" asked Rachel.

"I mean, it kinda adds up, doesn't it?"

"Ask Callie. She'd know," Talya said, rubbing a layer

of lip liner onto her finger and applying it to her lips in the mirror.

"What's that supposed to mean?" I asked. Of course, I knew what she meant, but the fact that she said it at all annoyed me to no end.

Rachel suddenly looked ashen. "Oh, are you . . . ? I didn't mean to offend you."

"You didn't," I said.

"I'm cool with it. We all are." Suddenly, six pairs of eyes were on me, as though I owed all of them an explanation or a show or something.

"That's awesome," I said. I popped the toothbrush into my mouth and started brushing vigorously, focusing intently on the sudsy reflection in the metal. I wasn't going to give them the satisfaction of an explanation.

"Leave her alone. It's none of anyone's business," Riley said, which I appreciated. I was beginning to see her as a separate person from her bestie, Gracie. Initially I hadn't been able to see much difference. But I liked that she had a little more spine.

Gracie, who was still standing by the door, pointed a finger I my direction. "So that's why you said you weren't into Austin."

"Nope, has nothing to do with that," I said, my mouth full of toothpaste. Finally, I spit. Talya looked at me expectantly, waiting for me to tell all. I could tell it made her uncomfortable that everyone thought I was a lesbian.

"It's her moms. She has two moms. Well, I guess foster moms," Talya said, correcting herself. Why she never knew when to stuff a sock in it, I couldn't figure out.

"Ahh, now it makes sense. The juvie, the foster family. Got it," Gracie said. "No judgment, of course."

I rinsed my face and dried it. Gracie was not the kind of person I'd ever be close friends with, but I could tell she meant it. Not like someone who insults you and then adds "no offense" to somehow make it better. She really wasn't judging. With Talya, on the other hand, it was hard to tell.

"Cool," Kellan said. "That must be kind of interesting. So no dad around to scream his head off every time you get below an A minus? Seriously, if I had two moms, I think my ulcer pains just might go away." She didn't give any of us time to digest that information or respond before she picked up her makeup case and left the bathroom.

"Geez, drama much?" Talya said.

"You know, not everything requires a comment," I said. She was really getting on my nerves.

"What the hell crawled up your butt and died?" she said.

"I'm just saying, leave it alone sometimes. You don't . . . You just . . . I don't know. Whatever." Now it was my turn to leave. And I couldn't get out of there fast enough. Gracie was right on my heels.

I didn't much feel like talking about my moms or anything else, but I had a feeling Gracie knew that. "She seems like she can be a bit much to take sometimes," was all she said.

"You could say that."

"Well, it's fine. You can do your own thing with whoever you want tonight and steer clear of her. There are enough of us that you don't really have to deal with her if you don't want to." Gracie was practically loping along the pathway. Even with my flashlight, I was having trouble keeping up with her without tripping. I couldn't figure out why she was being so nice. Then I remembered she might want my help getting together with Austin, though I still had no idea how I could make that happen. Or if I even wanted to.

"I'm not sure I'm gonna sneak out with you guys. I'm really wiped and I may just stay on my bunk and read." I knew I sounded like a wet mop but I really was tired and if I was gonna get in trouble for sneaking out, I wanted it to be the next night, when I was fully prepared to leap electric fences and guard dogs if it meant getting to see Brandon.

Gracie looked at me like she was trying to figure me out. "You're the girl who's had probably the least sheltered life of any of us, and you're gonna stay in and read? How's that make sense?"

"Maybe I'm just tired of getting in trouble. I don't know."

"Yeah, I hear that," she said. "Well, listen, you're cool covering for me if it comes up somehow?"

"You were in our bunk all night long. Got it." Maybe that's all she wanted or needed. I felt relieved at the thought.

"I'm not gonna do anything too naughty. Except maybe a magical brownie or two."

"You brought pot?"

"Shhh. Not that you know about," she said with a wink.

It was darker outside than I'd seen in a long time. Tons of stars had come out and I swear there were more of them than I'd ever seen before. For the first time, I caught a glimpse of what Lena had been talking about when she'd told me she envied me getting to see the world outside of my world. I took a deep breath and felt myself relax. It was hard to feel too self-important out there with a million stars reminding me how small I really was.

"So you're really gonna be a homebody tonight? Sure you don't wanna come party with us? It'll be fun. You don't have to drink if you're not into that," Gracie said.

"It's not that. I just . . . kinda want to be mellow tonight. Rain check?" I had no doubt there would be another party. Gracie high-fived me.

"Definitely." We were back at our tent and somehow Talya had beat us back. She had put on a tank top with a long red scarf wrapped around her neck. She looked pretty and vulnerable and I felt a little sorry for her. She was just trying to fit in, but somehow that always ended up feeling like she was trying to one-up me.

I stood outside our tent and took a last look up at the sky before turning in for the night. The longer I looked, the more stars I could make out.

Austin appeared out of nowhere. Even in the dark, his knowing grin and flashing eyes found me before I had a chance to prepare myself. "You coming down to the lake?" he asked me.

"Maybe later," I said, pushing through the tent flap door before he had a chance to convince me otherwise. Talya slid past me and grabbed Austin's arm, ready to go wherever he was taking her. Her voice went up an octave when she talked to him, more feminine and squeaky, if that was even possible.

"Wait up, 'k? I just need a jacket," she told him.

"I don't mind keeping you warm," I heard Austin say. Giddy, Talya came into the room with her cheeks flushed. She shuffled through her bag, looking for a sweater. I thought about saying something to her about Austin, but what could I say, really? I barely knew him but I had a feeling he might not be the dream date Talya was hoping he would be.

Talya grabbed a bottle of water from her bag and

swished out the door. Better not to say anything and let her have some fun, I decided.

"Did you hear we're getting four points of credit for this weekend? That'll push me above a 4.0 in social studies," Riley said.

"You're a total brain. You're probably above a 4.0 anyway," Gracie said.

Riley looked like she'd been caught. "Okay, maybe, but I still need the points if I'm gonna try for Penn. What colleges are you interested in, Callie?"

I had been hoping she wouldn't ask. I hardly wanted to admit I needed this project to keep from flunking out. It wasn't really embarrassment; I just didn't want to bore them with my whole tale. "I'm, um, still thinking about it," I said.

"I get that. Only some people have been planning for college since seventh grade," Gracie said, looking at Riley.

"Whatever. I have a goal. Could be worse," Riley said.

"I think it's awesome you know what you want to do," I said. "I'm just not quite there yet." I needed the conversation to end. True, I needed this weekend project to go well if I wanted to go to college, but was that even what I wanted? I couldn't honestly say. I waited for Riley and Gracie to sneak out of our room and leave me to figure it all out. Or just wallow on my own.

Chapter 8

I couldn't sleep. I think it was the chorus of crickets that I couldn't be sure were actually outside our tent. They were loud enough that I was pretty sure one was right under my bed. I had moved about an hour earlier from the bottom bunk to the top, just in case crickets could jump that high. Now it was about ten degrees hotter on the top bunk and it was after one a.m. Riley and Gracie had come back over an hour earlier, saying the hang by the lake was pretty lame. Max and Jaden had tried to sneak some beer from their bags and bring it down to the lake, but Bryce had beaten them to the punch. Obviously he wasn't new to the whole idea of kids sneaking out to party. Gracie said he was camped out by the lake and planning to sleep there in a sleeping bag with no tent. You couldn't pay me enough to do that. I imagined bugs crawling all over me and shuddered.

He was cool about everyone being out past curfew, and hung out until close to midnight before walking everyone back to the tents. So any illicit activity was out, but Riley said everyone still had fun. I felt like a loser for staying in the tent, but I figured I needed to earn some good-girl points if I wanted to be above suspicion the next night, when I would definitely be sneaking out to meet Brandon. No idea how I was going to do that when Bryce seemed determined to stay a step ahead of us, but I'd figure out a way.

What I couldn't figure out was what had happened to Talya. She still wasn't back and Gracie said she hadn't seen her by the lake. Austin either. Gracie and Riley mostly hung with Max and Jaden, played some cards, snuck a sip from a flask Jaden stashed in his jacket pocket, and eventually came back to the tent. "So what about Talya and Austin? Where were they? What were they up to?" I couldn't help asking again.

"I dunno. Why so obsessed?" Gracie asked. "I thought you weren't into him."

"Not obsessed. And I'm not into him. I just wondered how they managed to evade the all-seeing eye of Bryce."

"Oh, I'm sure they found a way. From what I hear about Austin, he knows how to work it."

I wanted to know what she meant by that. What was his story? I knew I already sounded like I was overly interested, or even obsessed, so I let it go. But I couldn't stop thinking about Talya and Austin and what they were doing. The two of them had managed to steal away somewhere without Bryce noticing, and I wasn't sure when I should switch from being annoyed by her to being worried.

I didn't have to debate too long, because I heard footsteps outside the tent door a couple of minutes later. No voices, just shuffling feet. I poked my head up to see Talya stumble into the room. In the glow of the moonlight, I glanced outside, expecting to see Austin standing there with that lazy smile, but there was no one. Had he bailed without walking her back in the middle of the night?

"Hey, you okay?" I whispered. She didn't answer. She had her back to me and lurched from the doorway back outside without closing the tent door. I could hear the even breathing of Gracie and Riley and didn't want to wake them, so I slid down from the top bunk and slipped out the tent door, closing it behind me. Then I used my flashlight to keep track of Talya as she made her way down the path to the bathrooms. Jamie was right. It was a long walk. A swarm of bugs flitted around the bare bulb outside the bathroom, making a dull humming sound. Other than that, it was totally quiet.

I went into the bathroom. "Talya, hey. How'd it go tonight? You have fun?" She didn't answer. "Talya?"

I could see her feet in the stall, facing the toilet. I wondered if she was going to be sick.

"Do you need anything? I'm just checking," I said.

Finally, I heard her muffled voice. "I'm good. You can go back to bed."

She didn't sound like herself. "Are you sure? I can, you know, stay here a while if it would make you feel better."

"It wouldn't," she said quickly. Her voice sounded strained, like she was trying to choke back tears. A big brown moth had landed on the sink next to me and I inched away, feeling like it was bound to jump on me if I didn't get out of there. And Talya made it clear she didn't want company.

"Fine. Okay, if you're sure." I didn't want to leave her in there. I could tell something wasn't right.

Abruptly, she unlocked the door to the stall and blew past me. "I said I was fine. Right?"

"Sure. Right." She stormed out of the bathroom and started walking unsteadily up the path back to the tent. I stayed behind for a minute and watched her. She looked drunk—or confused—or something. But she was managing to make her way back. So I took my flashlight and walked back. It was close to two a.m. and my eyes were burning. When I got back to the tent, Talya was passed out on her bunk, still wearing her clothes and shoes. Whatever explanation she had would have to wait until morning.

Chapter 9

All I can say is that the little talk Jamie and Bryce had with us about teamwork and the importance of our "living planet" did nothing to prepare us for what we faced on Saturday. We're talking boulders on our shoulders and no sign of a break. Jamie took her team, which included my bunk and a couple of the guys from tent seven, up a huge hill, scrambling through low, scraggly bushes instead of walking on a trail like normal people. It was probably eighty-five degrees in the shade, of which there was none.

"I thought this was supposed to be a forest project," Riley said. "Where are the trees?"

"It's run by the forest service, but this project doesn't

actually take place in the heart of a forest," Jamie said. "We'll get to an area with some trees later on. But right now, we're working on the slope."

"More like a desert," a guy named Keith grumbled.

"Isn't there, like, a trail we should be walking on? It seems like we're messing with the plants by trampling over them," I said. It wasn't just that I felt like I was killing plants as we tromped over them, but I also figured the chance of a snake or a swarm of wasps hiding under some bush was pretty great.

"Exactly!" Jamie said, like I'd discovered uranium. "There are no trails in this part of the state park, and we're here to build them. We need to dig in and set railroad ties on the steep parts and clear away the brush to make a trail."

"What's that over there? That looks like a trail. Maybe our work here is done," Keith said, pointing to a nearby hill where we could see a wide swath cutting through the brush.

"That's a firebreak. You can hike on it, sure, but it doesn't get you out of today's trail duty. You're here to work, right? No one's looking for an easy way out, are you?"

I guess she took the murmur of sarcasm that followed to mean we agreed with her plan, because she was hiking at top speed again, ushering us along behind her like baby chicks. I wondered where she got her energy and her boundless enthusiasm for sweating on a dirty "slope."

For a long time, we hiked in silence. We were nowhere near the top of the hill and I could feel a layer of trail dust on my teeth. Gracie wiped the sweat off her forehead and Riley pushed her sunglasses down to keep her steaming face from fogging them. But I had to hand it to them. They weren't complaining. Not nearly as much as Talya, who I'd gathered by now was pretty hungover. But she still wouldn't talk about what went down the night before, which was strange, since she'd been all too happy to tell everyone she planned to party. Maybe she was worried about Jamie finding out about whatever she'd been up to.

I took the opportunity to try to get some information out of her. Frankly, I was a little bit worried. "Hey," I said, moving away from the group a little bit so other people wouldn't overhear.

"Yeah?" She didn't look at me. And through her dark sunglasses, I couldn't read her expression.

"What happened last night?"

"What do you mean?"

"I dunno. It was just weird how you came in and left without saying anything."

"I didn't want to wake you," she said. She moved away from me but I wasn't going to let her get out of this that easily. That was one benefit of being out in the middle of nowhere: there was nowhere to hide.

"C'mon. You knew I was awake." I said, trying to make my voice sound as un-judgy as I could. "I just wanted to make sure you, you know, had help if you needed anything."

She took a step closer to me. "Thanks for that. But I didn't. Need anything. That's why I just went back to the bunks."

"So were you out partying with Austin?" She looked away and started pulling strands off one of the wild mustard plants next to us. I could smell the dry aroma of the spicy leaves. She shook her head.

"Nah, I wasn't really into his whole thing. I just hung with Jaden. He's really cool." For some reason, I felt relieved knowing she wasn't with Austin. It wasn't jealousy, or at least I didn't think so. I didn't know what it was. Hearing she was with Jaden put things in a different light. Still, I wasn't sure I believed her. Gracie and Riley had been with Max and Jaden all night and they hadn't mentioned Talya being there. Maybe she snuck off with Jaden later. I felt like I was reading tea leaves trying to figure out what Talya had been up to, and I wasn't sure I even cared.

"Yeah, Jaden seems like a good guy," I said. But not if he'd taken her somewhere and gotten her plastered. "What did you guys end up doing?"

Talya picked up a shovel and started chipping away at the dry dirt around a small plant that smelled like licorice. "Oh, he took me on a really long walk all around the lake. He's one of those people who kinda has a sixth sense about directions even though he's never been here before."

"So you guys just walked . . . and talked or whatever?"

"Definitely a little bit of whatever," she said, smiling to herself. "I think he was into it. I don't know, do you ever feel like you just can't read a guy even though you're making out with him?"

"If he's making out with you, it's probably a safe bet he's into you," I said. Talya blushed. I could tell she genuinely liked him. Maybe I was all wrong about her the night before. Maybe she wasn't drunk. More like drunk in love.

"I hope so. I feel like it needs to happen with the right guy for once." She looked at me, unspoken heaviness in her sigh. I knew how much it had hurt when Brandon broke up with her, and we'd only talked about it a little. I wondered if she wanted to get into all that now. Did I?

If she wanted to go deep with me here, I felt like I kind of had to let her. It's not that I thought I owed her anything because of the whole Brandon thing. But here she was putting it all out there and I couldn't just blow her off.

"I get that. That's kind of why I'm just doing my own thing for a while. I need it to be right. If it's gonna happen."

"Totally. Is that why you . . . ?"

"I don't really want to go into it. I mean, yeah, with Brandon there was just too much . . . you know. And with Wyatt, it got so intense." I wasn't sure why I was telling her this but it felt okay to like her a little bit. And to have her open up to me like a friend. We'd never really been on those terms before.

"So maybe there's the right balance. Maybe you'll meet him this weekend." She was watching Keith and Blake carry a series of rocks up the hill toward where we were working. Keith had rolled the sleeves of his T-shirt up to his shoulders to duck the heat, and there was no way not to check out his arms. They flexed each time he lifted a rock, and his sandy blond surfer hair kept falling in his face. He was wearing a red sports headband around his forehead but it didn't help much. Blake could not have been more the opposite type. He was wearing khaki shorts and a polo shirt, and looked like he'd just stepped out of some kind of catalog. "Just out of curiosity, which of those two did you have pegged for me?" I asked.

"Oh, I don't know. You seem like you'd be into Keith. He's got that whole rebel thing happening."

"What makes you think I'm into that?"

"I don't know." She smiled like we both knew.

"Is he your type?" I asked. It made me more comfortable to talk about Talya's love life than my own. She didn't seem to mind.

She looked him over and smiled. Then she kicked at the rocky dirt and didn't answer.

"Come on, tell me!"

"He's adorbs, right? But I'm pretty into Jaden after last night. This trip could turn out to be a game-changer, you know? Point us all in a different direction."

I thought about that. Maybe she was right. I'd been dreading this weekend since Lena told me about it, but looking at Jamie and her enthusiasm for the open road and hearing Talya talk to me like a real friend made me see why these trips out of our own realities could be a good thing. I noticed the heat had abated a little bit and a thick cover of clouds had formed overhead, not blocking out the blue of the sky, but blunting the glare of the sun a little bit.

I don't know how long I stood there daydreaming in my newfound enlightened state, but I was snapped out of it pretty quickly.

"Hey, you two, grab some shovels," Jamie said, pointing at Talya and me. "You're gonna start digging the footing for the landing."

I had no idea what that meant. "Where do you want us to dig?" I asked.

Jamie pointed to the area at her feet, which looked just about as random as anywhere else. "Right here. Dig a trench about a foot deep and two by four across and we can pop in the railroad ties and make a landing." She might as well have been speaking Chinese for all I understood. She made it sound so easy. It was hard to believe this was somehow comparable to going to school and taking a few tests.

But for the first time, I didn't mind. I was even a little bit psyched.

Chapter 10

"*Oh, I get what we're doing,*" I said. "This whole hill is going to be a stairway?" It was kind of cool. I'd only been hiking a few times, so I didn't know much about what a trail was supposed to look like. "I never really thought about how trails got here."

"I could make a crack about you being a city kid, but truth is, doesn't matter where you live," Jamie said. "If no one takes you out and sparks your appreciation, you can go years without ever looking up at the sky and really seeing it."

Somehow everything she said sounded poetic. "Were you always into hiking and stuff?"

"My mama used to take me camping. Nothing

strenuous—she was a big lady. Hiking definitely wasn't her thing. We'd drive into a campsite and pitch a tent right next to the car. But I learned early how to build a fire and cook outside."

"Are we gonna be doing that on this trip?"

"You want to learn how to build a fire? I can teach you. Food tastes better when you cook outside, I'll tell you that," she said. Despite her long dreadlocks and the extra weight she carried around, she never seemed winded and she looked completely comfortable in the heat.

"I wish I could learn to like it out here."

"Wishing's the first step," she said. And handed me a shovel that was nearly as tall as I was. The dirt was hard and after a winter with hardly any rain, the earth just didn't want to give. I could scrape a layer off the top, but to really get in there and move dirt, I had to stab at the dirt with the tip of the shovel at an angle. Even then, it would take me an hour to dig a foot down. Gracie wasn't even trying. She'd found a spot in the shade and waved me away when I tried to beckon her over to my dirt pile.

It was kind of nice to dig in peace for a while. Max and Austin were lugging bundles of railroad ties up to the site and going back down to the truck for more. I could hear them talking as their voices came closer. "I mean, we had fun last night, for sure. That girl likes a party," Austin said.

"Just be careful, man."

"Sounds like you believe the rumors."

I couldn't hear Max's response. They'd dumped their railroad ties on the piles and were heading back to the truck. I kept on scraping at the hardened earth, only partly interested in eavesdropping. I noticed for the first time how quiet it was, despite the couple dozen of us out there working. I could barely hear the voices of the kids up the hill and I had the sense that we were completely alone; no one around for miles, except maybe animals, and that freaked me out a little bit. I heard some birds but I listened carefully for the signs of any rustling. This could definitely be snake territory. The more I concentrated, the quieter it got and the more I was certain I could hear something. I just couldn't tell what. Could've been the wind, could've been my imagination. I looked down the path, hoping someone would come around and keep me company. The joy of solitude quickly lost its allure. I tried to focus on scraping the dirt off a big chunk of rock.

Max and Austin came back a few minutes later, still having the same conversation. "So what did you do? We didn't see you down by the lake," Max said.

"Aw, you know. Not cool to kiss and tell," Austin said. I saw him drop the pile of wood to the ground.

"Except you know you want to."

"Except you know I want to." I walked a few steps closer to where they stood. Safety in numbers. "She was cool. I dunno, you know. Just a fun time, that's all."

"She seems like a nice girl, Talya. Like I said, be careful. She doesn't seem like the kinda girl who's just up for a party."

"Not how it looked last night. But why are you so interested? You jealous? You have her in mind for yourself?"

"Not at all. I'm just sayin'."

"'Cause I'm pretty much done with her after last night. She's all yours."

"Dude, I didn't say I wanted in. I just meant, you know, don't mess with her mind too much."

I wondered if I'd heard them right. Did Austin say he was with Talya? She'd spent half the morning talking about the night she spent with Jaden. Nothing added up. Then again, Austin liked to talk a good game, so I couldn't really take what he said to mean all that much.

I walked over to where they were still talking, seeming to forget about the job of lugging railroad ties. My plans for overhearing any more about Austin's travails the night before were quashed when they abruptly started talking about sports.

"Hey, anyone ready for a break?" I asked.

Austin leveled me with those eyes. But after hearing the way he talked about the girl he had been with, his eyes just looked manipulative. "Callie. What's up?"

"Just doing my digging, earning my feeble community service points through hard labor." I looked at the pile of railroad ties. "Are we supposed to start setting these in?"

Max picked one up. "I wanted to get a bunch of them up here before we laid them into the ground, but we've got a whole pile now." He gestured around to the scattered planks of wood, looking proud of his effort.

"Great, let's do it. Do you know how to put them in?" I asked. Secretly, I was hoping to have some help digging out the spaces where the wood steps needed to go and Max and Austin would definitely get that accomplished in half the time I could. I walked them back to the bottom of the trail where I'd been digging.

"Wait, you didn't dig out the footings yet," Austin said.

"I started," I said, pointing to my sad effort at digging.

"Uh-huh." Austin turned and headed back down toward the truck. "Nice try, girlfriend, but I'm not doing your work for you. Unless you make it worth my while." He turned and winked. Max shrugged but didn't follow Austin right away.

"What's his deal?" I asked.

Max didn't say anything. But he didn't leave, either. I could tell he knew more than he was saying.

"C'mon, spill it," I said.

"I mean, I barely know the guy. This is all by reputation and rumor and half of it probably isn't true, so I shouldn't be spreading it."

"Yeah, yeah, I know. You're a good guy and you don't

want to get caught up in rumors and all that. Don't worry, whatever you say is in the vault with me." I stared him down, not wanting him to chicken out of telling me what he knew.

Max looked pained at the idea of talking, but he didn't walk away. I noticed how blue his eyes were now in the daylight. They were pale, like the color of the sky, and they made him look innocent.

"I'm pretty sure he's not here for regular extra credit like the rest of us, put it that way."

"I still don't know what that means."

"What I heard was that some of the kids at his school were cheating. Stealing tests and stuff. And all of them got suspended except him."

"Well, maybe he wasn't one of the ones cheating."

Max hesitated like this couldn't possibly be true. "That or . . ."

"What?"

"He worked the system somehow. Ratted people out to save his own ass. That's why he got community service instead of a full-on suspension. I don't know. I shouldn't be spreading rumors when I don't know the real story."

"It's okay. I asked. And I won't say anything to anyone else."

Max nodded. "Cool." He picked up my shovel and started digging where I had been struggling. The dirt seemed to ease up under the pressure of his shoulders and he flung it away in huge chunks.

"Maybe I should be lugging railroad ties and you should be digging. You're a lot better at it than I am."

"You just need to get your back into it. Really lean when you put the shovel down." I tried it his way and sure enough, a little more dirt came loose. Not as much as when he did it, but it was something.

"You have a lot of experience with hard labor?" I asked.

"I just lift weights and stuff, so I know how to shift my body weight to accomplish what I need without hurting something." He wasn't bragging. The way he said things was just him stating a fact, disseminating information because it was true. I could tell he worked out, but it had to be for a sport he played. He didn't seem like the kind of guy who just pumped iron for show.

"They should have offered all of us that kind of boot camp before we came," I said as I looked down at my own definition-less arms.

"Really? You would have done that kind of boot camp?"

I laughed at the thought. "Yeah, you're right. Probably not." He dug into the soil again and hefted another huge pile out of the ground with barely any effort. "So you think I can just move mountains like that if I put my weight into it?" I asked, highly skeptical.

He sized me up, too polite to say anything about my barely-there biceps. "Let's give it a try." He handed me the shovel and showed me how to angle it into the soil. The tip barely budged a spoonful of dirt. "See, it's kinda futile," I said.

"No, but here's where the magic happens. Put your foot on it and literally stand on it with all your weight." I hopped on the flat edge of the shovel and was surprised to find that it sunk about six inches into the ground. "Now jump off and lean on the handle. Put all your weight on it." I did and an impressive clump of dirt dislodged. I could see the soil beneath it had a few rocks but it looked less dry and foreboding.

"See, it's hard-packed on top and really dry, but once you get under that top layer, you'll get a little more movement and you won't have to work as hard." I looked at him and smiled, impressed by his intuitive understanding of how to move dirt. "What?" he asked, looking concerned.

"I'm just impressed with the whole John Muir thing you've got going."

"I'm impressed you know who John Muir is." Now he was smiling, too. If you didn't know better, you'd think we'd known each other for longer than a day.

"What are you two lovebirds so happy about?" Austin asked, dumping another couple of wood chunks at our feet. "Did I miss something when I was back there actually working?"

"We're starting on the stairway," Max said. "Should we see how far we can get with the railroad ties we have here before we get more from the truck?"

Austin sat down on the trunk of a fallen tree and wiped the sweat out of his eyes, which made them glisten in an even more intense shade of green. "Yeah, that or we take a little breather. I don't see Jamie or Bryce here checking us out, so I say we chill." I had no problem with that idea. I sat down on the log and Max plunked down between Austin and me, but he kept a safe distance between us. I wondered if he was uncomfortable around me with Austin there.

I realized for the first time I was clammy with sweat, as rivulets ran down under my shirt. There wasn't much in the way of shade. Austin must've been thinking the same thing, because he pointed to the log where we were sitting. "I heard there was some kind of beetle disease that swept through here. Killed a bunch of trees."

"Yeah, I remember reading about that. The ones that didn't die like this one were clear-cut, 'cause they were worried about them falling and blocking roads and stuff."

"So that's why we're on this mission to plant new trees," I said. Suddenly, it all made sense. Lack of shade and all.

"Um, yeah. That's pretty much the whole point of this project. Did you not get the memo?" Max teased.

"I didn't exactly read up," I said.

Our rest hour was short-lived, because Jamie came up from out of nowhere and busted us for sitting around. "Hey, people, there's a stairway to build here and I don't see it building itself."

"Ugh," I complained. "It's so hot. Can't we do this when it cools down a bit?"

"We'll be working then, too. I told you to wear a long-sleeved white shirt, didn't I?" It's true. She'd told me that the night before, but I hadn't listened.

"Yeah, but it's a million degrees out here. I figured short sleeves would be cooler." I looked down and saw that my red shirt was stained with a river of sweat. Very becoming.

I looked at Jamie and noticed her loose-fitting white shirt, made of such light cotton it actually seemed to be floating on the breeze. Her khaki shorts also had an airy quality about them. Under her big bucket hat, she was barely breaking a sweat, and here the rest of us were cooking out in the sun. I realized I should be taking my cues directly from her. She clearly knew what she was doing. "The long sleeves actually keep you cooler. Having the sun beating down on your skin is what makes you hot. White reflects."

"Whatever, man. It's a hundred degrees out here. I don't think there's anything that's gonna keep us cool except an air-conditioned van. You got one of those?" Austin asked.

"We'll get back in the vans soon and head down to the main site for lunch." She looked at her watch. I didn't know anyone still wore a watch. But Jamie was the kind of person who didn't do what everyone else did just because it was the most common way to go about things. "About twenty more minutes till noon. So work hard these next few, see if you can get eight more steps laid in before we head down."

I looked at the hill and the pile of wood. Eight more steps seemed like a lot, but I liked that we had a goal. And the incentive of lunch. Max and Austin must've felt the same way, because they started digging and hoisting railroad ties at a faster pace.

Jamie headed back up to where I could see Talya and Riley carrying more tools down the path. I saw Austin looking after them and decided to tackle the subject of the previous night myself. "So, I know I was a shut-in last night, but did you get your party?"

Austin stretched like my question just made him realize how tired he was from the late night. "Oh, yeah. It was epic."

"Who'd you hang with?"

"Your girl Tals. Man, she's a live one." I looked him in the eye, trying to figure out if he was telling the truth. He smirked like he knew he was stirring up trouble between us. "She may be a little worse for the wear today, though. Girl's gotta learn her limits."

"I wouldn't know. We're not super close," I said, the wheels spinning in my head while I weighed the possibilities. Had I spent the whole morning opening up to someone who was lying right to my face?

Chapter 11

Turns out Jamie was kidding about the air-conditioned van. We had a long walk back to the main site with Bryce while she sped back in the truck.

"Hey, no fair," Jaden said when he saw her pull out her keys.

"I'm gonna make lunch for two dozen people who've been working all morning and try to get it done before you get down to camp. Still sound like a cakewalk to you?"

"No, sounds like you should be getting paid. A lot," Max said. Jamie laughed and gave him a thumbs-up.

We started down the trail, which mercifully began to wind through a stand of actual trees. I hadn't been able to see this part from where we were working, but after hearing about how many trees the beetles had destroyed, I was glad to see that a good part of the forest still existed. Still, the further we walked into what felt like a normal forest, the more clearly I could see why the forest service needed our help out there.

"Once we reforest the stretch of land back there, the birds will come back, the animals will repopulate the area. A whole ecosystem will renew itself," I heard Bryce telling a group behind me.

Austin sidled up next to me. "These people never quit. I had no idea this was gonna be some kind of cultish, happy forest thing. They're not gonna be happy till we're all making a love circle in the forest and groping trees." I ignored him. Or tried to. His presence still had the same effect on me, a chill and a nervous flutter in my stomach, even though my brain reminded me the last thing I needed in my life right then was another guy. Especially a guy like him. I just wished he wasn't so ridiculously hot.

I walked a little faster and caught up with Riley and Gracie, who were talking about some fashion Web site I'd never heard of. "OMG, did you see what they posted this week in the gotta-have column?" Riley said.

"You mean the black dress? Seriously, so cute!"

"It's not a dress. It's a romper."

"Okay, please don't call it that. Makes it sound like something I wore when I was two."

"I know, right? I guess it's because it's not really a dress. It's got legs like shorts." I had no idea what they were talking about. I was just glad to be relieved of digging and needed something to pass the time on the walk back. And I wanted some time to think about the Talya situation. I couldn't figure out why she'd lied when it finally felt like we'd broken through to maybe becoming friends. Could it have something to do with Brandon? Maybe she still didn't trust me. Like she thought if she said she liked Austin, maybe I'd try to swoop in and destroy everything. Again. Or maybe it had nothing to do with me. Maybe she'd done things with Austin she regretted and she was lying to protect herself. And there was always the very good possibility that Austin had made the whole thing up. I couldn't decide whether to hate Talya or feel sorry for her.

"Wait, what Web site?" And there she was. Talya wasn't one to miss out on a conversation she thought might be important.

Riley and Gracie had stopped to check out the exposed roots of a tree that had fallen over. The tangled mane of thick roots looked like its own kind of art form, reaching away from the trunk of the tree in a confused bundle. Gracie perched on the horizontal trunk and Riley snapped a photo with a disposable camera. Talya swung a leg over the tree trunk and posed next to Gracie. "Get one of both of us." Riley complied.

"We were talking about Stylebop.com, you know, the fashion site with all the, like, huge discounts?" Gracie said. "I'm telling you, Ri, that romper or whatever you want to call it would look amazaballs on you." Riley blushed and looked at the ground. She seemed uncomfortable, but I couldn't figure out why. She started walking again, leaving Talya and Gracie back by the tree, talking about their clothing allowances. "I get a grand per season to spend on whatever I want," Gracie said.

"Wow. I wish I could just have free rein like that. My mom, like, has to be in on every decision I make. But then she pretty much lets me spend whatever I want."

"See, so there's a good and a bad."

I'd lost interest, so I picked up my pace and caught up with Riley.

I should've known our walk back to camp for lunch was too good to be true. About twenty minutes in, Bryce had us stop in a small clearing where it looked like a tree massacre had taken place. In the middle of the forest, where large fir and pine trees towered overhead, this was a stretch of charred earth and blight that looked wrong. Something had happened here. Something lethal to all the once-living plants. It kind of looked like a burned-up moon.

"Brush fire destroyed this area a few years back," Bryce

said, unzipping his backpack. "You can see it's starting to come back in patches." I looked around and could see some sprigs of grass off in the distance, but that was about it.

"I wouldn't say it's making much of a comeback," Jaden said.

Bryce pulled out a big baggie of what looked like black plastic test tubes. He untied the knot in the bag and spilled the tubes out onto the ground. "Grab a few, each of you. We'll divide into groups and get these planted."

"What are they?" I asked.

"Seedlings. Pine and fir, mostly. But there's some manzanita in there, too. Doesn't matter which ones you choose. Just take a handful." He pointed to an area where the dirt had already been turned. I silently rejoiced at the idea of no more digging.

"Normally, an area like this would repopulate itself with new plants. Grasses, then shrubs, eventually trees. But the beetle population destroyed the seed pods, so it's up to us to replant the area."

Everyone was focused on the devastated land around us. Maybe they felt the same awe that I did, realizing we had the power to change the landscape. We would literally be changing the planet. Not to sound too grandiose, but if you thought about it, we were saving a little bit of it. I took a deep breath and realized I didn't breathe like this at home, even though we lived by the ocean and the air had always seemed clean. It was different here, cleaner and lighter somehow. I felt the air pull into my lungs, and instead of exhaling right away, I kept on inhaling, like the air just kept going and going, which felt strange and awesome at the same time.

Bryce divided us into groups. I was grateful when he pulled me into a group with two guys I hadn't worked with yet, Charlie and Josh, who were Asian American twins. They went to Anchor Prep, like most of the others, and I'd seen them playing volleyball that morning before breakfast. Both were tall and lanky with arms that went on forever, but when they set the ball and spiked it over the net, I could see their natural skills. There was something graceful about the way each jumped for the ball and arced an arm up to send it down over the net.

We carried our tiny plants to an area of dirt and started looking at where we could plant them. "How far apart should we space them?" Charlie asked.

"Bryce said to give them a foot at least," I said. "But if you think about them growing into trees, doesn't that seem too close together?"

"Natural selection," said a voice behind me. I turned to see Austin and Talya on my heels. I must've looked at him accusingly, because Austin put his hands up in defense. "Bryce sent us to join you."

"Right. Okay," I said, wondering if it was true. I got the feeling Austin did whatever he felt like, whether or not it annoyed everyone else. He liked to stir the pot and I felt even more determined not to let him get to me.

"Bryce was just telling us that some of the seedlings won't make it to full trees. Only like one in six will be here after a year," Talya said.

I looked down at my handful of seedlings, wondering which, if any of them, would make it to a full-sized tree. "I kind of feel bad for some of these," I said.

"I know, it's like they're our little babies and I want them all to grow up to be trees," she said. She came right over and started planting her seedlings next to me. I looked at Austin again for signs of tension. Maybe he'd been lying before and she was just planting next to me, not as a safe haven but just because she felt like being here. Austin was working with the guys and joking around, seeming completely disinterested in us.

"Maybe there's a way we can take care of them so they're more likely to survive. Should I ask Bryce if there's anything we can do? Maybe plant them further apart so they have more room?"

"I know. It seems like planting them close together will make them compete for the same water and, you know, resources or whatever." I was sounding like a science textbook, but something about seeing these little sprigs of pine was hitting a soft spot in me. I didn't want to think about them dying.

Talya called Bryce over. "Why do we have to assume

some of these plants won't make it? Can't we help them along?" she asked.

Bryce smiled. "I get what you're saying. It's not like you're dooming them just based on the statistics." He picked up one of the seedlings and brushed the dirt away from the roots. The delicate way he handled them made it seem like he cared more about them than we did. "It's just nature's way. As it is, we're trumping nature by doing the planting ourselves. If we can get half of these to grow into hearty trees, it'd be a big success. Don't get hung up too much on the ones that won't make it." He scooped away a patch of dirt and popped the seedling into place and covered the roots back up with soil. "Some of them don't have the genetic ability to thrive and it's right for them to be weeded out. Darwin and all," he said. He dropped down a box of a couple dozen more seedlings and moved off toward another group, calling back to us, "I'm just glad you care. You two have an open invitation any time to come join us out here."

I looked at Talya. She had a look on her face that was somewhere between amusement and total terror at the thought. We both burst out laughing as soon as he was out of range. "Okay, I just want the trees to grow, but I'm not looking to make a career of this."

"I hear that," I said. I planted a couple of seedlings myself, imitating the way Bryce had brushed the dirt off the roots and separated them before tucking them into the soil and scooping more dirt around to stabilize them. "Just get me through this weekend, is all."

"Did you hear we have to write a twenty-page report?" Talya asked.

"Shut up. I know Lena said something about a paper, but nothing about twenty pages."

"She probably knew if she told you, you'd bail."

I wanted to like Talya and I wanted to believe she was becoming my friend, someone who wouldn't lie about where she had been the night before. I studied her for a minute. On the surface, she looked vulnerable, the kind of person who wore her emotions right where you could see them.

"You feeling okay after last night? Hungover or whatever?" I broached the subject carefully, waiting for her response.

"Oh, yeah, all good." I studied her for signs she felt weird around Austin. But she wasn't watching him out of the corner of her eye or even remotely aware of him, still joking around with Charlie and Josh. If anything, I was the one who kept stealing glances his way, even though I couldn't really say why. I decided she was telling the truth and Austin, as I'd suspected, was not to be trusted. The evidence was piling up against him.

Of course, no sooner had I concluded that than he jumped over a log and came to plant the rest of his seedlings with us. *"Hola, chiquitas."* He sat down on the log and quickly dug out little patches and stuck his plants in without really looking at what he was doing.

"I think you're supposed to separate the roots," I said. Then I wondered why I was bothering to correct him. Maybe his plants would be the ones to die and ours would survive. I liked the idea of the statistics favoring us.

Talya was focused on her planting, the sweat rolling off her forehead. She wiped it off with her sleeve, not able to touch her face with her soil-covered hands. Austin had no more plants in his box, so he plopped down on the ground next to me and put his arm around my shoulder, leaning in. "Can I tell you something?" he asked.

His arm made me uncomfortable. But I didn't tell him to move it. "Sure, what's up?"

"I'm not an outdoorsy person." For some reason, that made me laugh. The left side of his mouth tipped up into a smile. "Okay, fine, so I guess I'm stating the obvious." He actually looked a little embarrassed. And just like that, all the cocky bravado slipped away and I felt myself start to like him.

"It's not that. It's just . . . this is about the last place I'd have pictured myself about a week ago," I said.

"Yeah. But I kinda like it here. I guess it's hard not to, right?" His shy smile made him appear self-conscious and he looked away. He seemed like a normal person, not someone who was trying to charm me or work an angle.

"Yeah, I get that. It's like you can just let go of the

regular life stuff and just, like, be," I told him. He raised his eyebrows. "Okay, that was really crunchy." I laughed again.

"Yup, you've got some legit flower power in there." Maybe it was just a question of getting through Austin's posturing to get to the regular guy. A guy I could actually like, provided he stayed that way. He grabbed a couple of my seedlings and brushed the soil off their roots, like I'd done. "Here, let's get these in the ground so we can go to lunch."

The next twenty minutes flew by and we got all our seedlings planted. Bryce herded us all together and we made our way back down toward camp. Austin was walking next to me and I noticed Talya lagging behind the group, staring at the ground while she walked. I yelled back to her and motioned for her to come up and join us, but she looked at me and looked away. Just when I'd thought we were making progress.

Chapter 12

I never thought I'd be so happy to see a tray of beige meats and cheese glistening in the heat. Part of me suspected there was a 50/50 chance of getting salmonella, but it seemed worth it. After a few hours of digging and lugging stuff in the hot sun, I was starved.

Two slices of dry bread and some mustard later, I took a bite of my sandwich and pushed the pile of chips around on my plate to make room for a huge wedge of watermelon from an oval platter on our picnic table. Then I grabbed one more piece. "Hungry much?" It was Max. He sat down next to me, closer than most people would have but, again, not so close that I felt like moving away.

"Crazy hungry. Who'd have thought you could work up such an appetite digging a hole?"

"It's the best kind of workout. Manual labor. Forget about gym rats or whatever. If you just do physical work, you'd never have to lift a barbell."

"Right. Lifting barbells. Two words that never enter my vocabulary," I said amid a mouthful of sandwich. Despite the mustard, it was dry and getting practically toasted in the heat. "Are you a big jock?"

"Well, when you ask it that way, I'm not sure I want to answer." I suddenly became aware I was checking him out. He had a near-perfect athlete's body. I hadn't meant to look him over that way and I immediately averted my eyes, hoping he hadn't noticed.

When I looked back at him, he was smiling like I'd been caught. "Okay, so you're like captain of the water polo team? Or head rowing guy?"

"Rowing guy? No, I'm a lacrosse player. And you definitely aren't a prep."

"Um, did you not hear my whole description of my life—multiple foster homes, juvie, long list of people in social services who know my name by heart?"

He looked embarrassed. "I wasn't—"

I held up a hand. This had the potential to get worse by the second. "Truce. I'm not offended by your lack of knowledge of the system. Just don't hold it against me if I don't know all the positions on the lacrosse team."

"Understood. How about if I educate you?"

"Does it require me to sweat any more than I already am?" He stood up and pulled a ball out of his pocket. How come athletes always happen to have sporting equipment handy even when they don't need it? He nodded vehemently at me.

"Oh, I'm afraid it does. Welcome to your first lacrosse lesson." He tossed the ball in the air and caught it without even looking up. He looked around at a pile of sports equipment near the building. "We brought some sticks. Never know when there's extra time to train, and we've got nationals coming up in a few weeks."

I looked at him with skepticism. "And I should know what 'nationals' are?"

He tossed the ball up in the air a couple more times, catching it easily with one hand before tossing it to me. I, of course, missed it and had to run after it as it rolled across the ground. I kept my eye on it, not wanting to see who might be watching my klutzy moves. And did I really care anyway? Not really.

"Again," he said. "Try to get into a rhythm. Throw and catch."

I tried. Throwing horribly and failing to catch. Again and again.

Annoyed at myself, I grabbed the ball and hurled it toward Max, who stuck a lacrosse stick up in the air and caught it as easily as a butterfly flying right into his net.

He handed me a stick and backed up. Then he tossed the ball that was in the basket of his stick toward me. I waved my stick around frantically, trying to position it anywhere near where the ball was whizzing toward me. The ball hit the basket and fell to the ground at my feet. Still, I was trying to feel the rhythm despite the obvious fact that I had none. So I picked up the ball and popped it in the basket of my own stick and hurled it with the same motion toward Max, who didn't make any moves toward catching it. I couldn't understand why he was just standing there—until it occurred to me that I didn't see the ball anywhere. That's when I looked up at my stick and realized the ball hadn't left the basket and I was probably hopeless at my new sport.

"Okay, thanks for the lesson, but I think I should spend a little time practicing on my own before I inflict my awesome athleticism on you or anyone else."

"C'mon, that was only one try. First time I tried throwing I hit myself in the head. You gotta give it at least an hour before you start to feel it."

"Yeah. Maybe when it cools down later." I retreated to the safety of my picnic bench, where there was still half a plate of watermelon. I watched Max and Jaden toss the ball back and forth easily, like the lacrosse sticks were part of their anatomy.

I appreciated that even though Max was clearly a standout player, going to nationals and all, he didn't mind taking the time to toss the ball with a beginner.

I grabbed my water cup for a big gulp but it was empty. Before I could make a move to get more, Austin handed me his cup of water and sat down at the table.

"I haven't touched it. Just so you know. In case you're like a germophobe or something."

I didn't have time to thank him; I just nodded as I slugged down gulp after gulp and drained it dry. "This round's on me," I said. I went over to the cooler and got more water. When I turned to head back to the table, I saw that Austin's eyes hadn't left me.

Talya was walking with her plate and I gestured for her to come over and join us, but she looked away, then started glancing around, like she hadn't really seen me. But I knew she had. I went back and sat with Austin, who had eaten about half my chips in the time it took me to get the water. "Thief!"

"I'll replace them, don't worry."

"You better. With interest." He laughed and grabbed a few more chips.

I looked around at what everyone else was doing, always feeling a little self-conscious around Austin. It's not like I thought anyone was interested in what I was doing, but I knew I had a tendency to forget the world around me sometimes and I wanted to make sure the whole group wasn't gathering for the next hike up the mountain without us. Austin wouldn't care, but I did.

Everyone was doing their own thing. A handful of people were playing volleyball and another small group had brought out poker chips and cards. I kept bracing myself for the moment when these private school kids would default to some kind of wealthy behavior I wouldn't be able to relate to. I kept expecting someone to out me as the one person there who didn't measure up to expectations. But so far, they just acted like everyone I knew from Anchor Beach, making me realize that maybe I was the one with preconceived ideas and expectations, which made me feel like a jerk.

A light cover of clouds had rolled in and blocked out the fiercest of the sun's rays, which would be a merciful change that afternoon when we went back out to do more digging or planting or whatever Bryce and Jamie had in store for us. I looked back at Austin, who was stacking the remaining potato chips into what looked like a tower.

"Are you just testing gravity there?" I asked.

"No, I was just waiting for you to come out of your fog and notice. You know you've been in a daze for like five minutes, right?"

"Sorry. I guess the morning took more out of me than I thought. I actually feel like I could take a nap right here."

"Go for it," he said, and backed away so I could have some space on the bench. I was tempted. Suddenly, a wave of exhaustion had overcome me. Maybe it was the morning's work, but more likely it was all the stresses of school and home and everything I'd been feeling for months beginning to rumble to the surface and make me notice that I was pretty worn out.

But I wasn't going to take a nap out there. Not with Austin staring down at me and smiling that smile.

"What?" I asked.

He shook his head. "I don't know. There's something about you . . . I just don't know. Anyone ever tell you that?"

"Well, I don't really know what you're talking about, so . . . no."

He looked me over and nodded slowly. "Yeah, I think you do," he said.

"Look, I'm just happy you started acting like a normal person," I said. "I was worried I was going to have to hate you all weekend long."

"*Hate*'s a strong word."

"Yeah," I said. "But I'm over it now." I didn't exactly feel comfortable around Austin, but I decided I didn't need to avoid him. The early stuff was probably his own discomfort, which came out in the form of strutting around like a peacock. As I looked at him now, he seemed pretty harmless. And the gorgeous factor didn't hurt, either.

"Besides," he said, scooting closer, "how am I supposed to learn all your deep, dark secrets if you hate me?"

"Ha. Well, deep, dark secrets you are not getting. So

let's just get that straight right here." It was one thing for me to decide Austin wasn't so bad. It was another to actually trust him, which I didn't.

Just then a lacrosse ball came whizzing past me about six inches from my head. I looked up at where Max stood, grinning guiltily. I leaned over and grabbed the ball, but I didn't trust my aim to get it anywhere near him, so I got up and walked a few feet closer.

"You know you almost took my ear off," I said.

"It wasn't me, I swear," he said, pointing at Jaden. "This guy has a wild arm sometimes and I couldn't snag it in time." Jaden looked horribly guilty and busted Max for not shouldering some of the blame.

"Dude, you could've at least taken one for the team. Callie likes you," Jaden said, twirling his stick. "Sorry, Callie. I was trying to make this guy run his lazy ass a little bit. Who knew he'd just let it go and practically clock you in the head?" By now I was close enough that I had a fair amount of confidence in my aim and I tossed the ball back to Max, who swiped at it with his stick and caught it expertly.

"Yeah, yeah. Blame me, why don'tcha?" Max said. "You're the one with the unpredictable arm."

"Okay, guys, carry on. Just remember, I need all my body parts for whatever hard labor Jamie has planned for us, so if you knock me out, you get double duty on the trails," I said.

"Deal," Max said. He cocked his arm back and pretended to hurl it toward me. I knew he was kidding around, but I ducked anyway.

I went back over to the table where Austin was sitting, mainly to see if he'd made good on his promise to refill my plate of chips. I didn't sit back down. "Looks like they're cleaning up. Guess we're going back out to the dusty wilderness," I said, grabbing the plate, which he had mercifully refilled.

I noticed that Talya was still hanging by herself. She stood almost frozen, over by a tree, watching us.

Chapter 13

Obviously, something was bothering Talya, and I was worried it had something to do with me. She'd been avoiding me ever since Austin had started hanging around, but there were still a lot of missing clues about the night before, and it was seeming more and more like he had something to do with whatever had gone on. I went to where Talya was standing. "Hey," I said.

She flashed a big, overly enthusiastic smile. "Oh, hey. Great lunch, huh? Just what I want after working my ass off—a bunch of room-temperature meat. Does that even make sense, room temperature, when we're not in a room?" She was talking fast, seemingly self-conscious.

"You just gave me indigestion," I said, actually feeling

my stomach turn over the sandwich I'd scarfed down in about three minutes. Better not to think too much about it. "So anyway . . . Everything okay with you?"

"Um, sure, why?"

"You just seemed like you were avoiding coming over to where Austin and I were sitting. Didn't you want to hang with us?"

I saw Jamie start putting away the food. I knew that meant we'd be heading out soon to do more work on the trails. She and Bryce folded up the meats in plastic wrap and put them back in the cooler. I hoped they wouldn't be making an appearance later on at dinner.

"Oh, were you wanting a third wheel? I didn't know." Her voice caught on the last words. She was bumming and I needed to know why.

"What are you talking about? It's not like Austin and I are a couple. I was just having lunch with him." Bryce started walking around with a tray of cookies. I was tempted to follow him, but I didn't want Talya to think I was ditching her.

"Looked a little friendlier than that," she said pointedly.

"Well, it wasn't," I said. "We're just friends. And barely even that." I swear, I felt like I was constantly stepping around land mines when it came to Talya.

She looked back at where Austin was sitting at the table and shook her head. "He's staring right at you."

"You and I are standing in the same place. How do

you know he's not staring at you?" But more than that, why was this all such a big deal to her? "Do you, like, have a thing for Austin? I thought you were all about Jaden."

Talya sighed and sat down. She looked like she was fighting back tears. "I mean, sort of."

"Sort of what? Did something happen with Jaden? Or . . . ?" I didn't know what to make of any of it.

She didn't say anything for a minute. At first I thought she hadn't heard my question. Then she winced. "Jaden wasn't really a thing. Actually . . ." She kicked at the ground, and a small line of ants changed direction and scattered all different ways. "I wasn't totally . . . honest when you asked about last night."

"Okay."

She shook her head. "I was with Austin. It was . . . kind of intense."

"He can be a little intense," I said. I knew he had that side, but after he'd come around and acted like a human being toward me, I didn't know what to think. Apparently he had lots of sides. "Is that why you lied?" I asked her, laying it on the table. I wanted it out in the open. Talya had lied to my face and I needed her to admit it.

She looked sheepish. "I'm . . . sorry about that. I just wasn't ready to . . . talk about it."

Which made perfect sense. But then why talk at all? "So why'd you say you were with Jaden?"

"I don't know, okay?" She sounded exasperated and

looked at me accusingly, like I was the one who'd done something wrong. "I just needed to say something and that's what came out. I mean, face it, you and I weren't exactly close before this trip. I didn't owe you the truth."

That felt like a slap in the face but I let it go. I'd done a lot of that with Talya after she and Brandon broke up. When was I going to stop feeling responsible for everything? "I was just trying to be a friend," I said. "Last night, when I asked what happened."

It's strange what girls will do to each other in the face of guy drama. The mere presence of a guy brings out behavior in ourselves that we don't even expect or understand. "I know," she said quietly. But she didn't say more. It felt awkward, me just sitting there, like I was waiting for something I didn't even want or need in the first place. So I started to walk away. "I wanted to tell you, or at least . . . I wanted to talk. To someone," she called after me. It felt a little insulting, but I went back and sat down. In case she still wanted to talk. To someone.

But she didn't talk for a while. We just sat and I started to think maybe that was all we were going to do until Talya seemed to decide she was ready to tell me everything. "I got kind of drunk and . . . I don't remember everything that happened. I mean, stuff happened. I know that. I just don't remember all of it." That didn't sound good. And there was a big question hanging in the balance.

"Did you sleep with him?" She looked at me blankly. "You don't remember?"

Talya shook her head. "I mean, it wouldn't be bad if I did. It was about time."

"About time?" I didn't understand what she was implying at first. She'd only known him a day. But then it landed on me. "You mean you've never had sex before?" She looked at the ground. "And you may have had your first time last night with Austin but you don't remember?"

"No, no. I mean, there was Brandon. But no one since him, and like I said, it was just time. I needed to get over him." My mind was spinning with the implications of what she was telling me. And all I could think was that this was bad. Or potentially bad. "But it's not on him, whatever happened," she said.

"Of course it's on him. If he got you drunk, or gave you a date-rape drug or whatever—"

"Oh, no, it wasn't like that. I wanted it. I was just nervous, so I did a few shots. And we made out. And it was awesome. I just don't know how far it went. But it's all good. It was really, really good."

"How can you say that when you don't remember all of it?"

"Because I woke up feeling in love. And that can't be bad. Can it?"

"I guess not. I mean, not if you're happy." I wasn't sure about any of it. And I had to tread delicately here. But my mind was reeling, unwelcome memories of Liam forcing their way back into my mind. I pushed the thoughts down, feeling a surge of nausea as I did and focusing as hard as I could on Talya. The here and now.

Talya was looking at me expectantly. She knew I had more to say. "I'm just not sure Austin is . . . He seems like the kind of guy you should be careful of. He's a charmer, but I'm not sure I trust him." Which was an understatement. Even if he'd shown me a nicer side, I couldn't be sure Austin hadn't taken advantage of Talya, especially when he had been talking smack earlier about her being a partier. Didn't sound like the love part had washed over him in quite the same way it had for her. Then again, guys have a funny way of showing it sometimes.

All the awkward conversations a random assortment of adults had tried to have with me ran through my head. "Did you, you know, use condoms or whatever?" I couldn't believe I was asking, but Talya seemed so clueless. There was probably a world of wrong in what had gone down that night.

She shook her head. "I'm on the pill."

"Why are you on the pill if you're not dating—"

She waved a hand at me to dismiss the conversation. "From before. I just . . . stayed on it." I decided not to get into the whole discussion about why she should still use a condom. Save that for some sex ed class she'd apparently flunked.

"Callie, you don't have to worry about me. I like that he seems a little dangerous."

"So you're . . . good with this?" I asked. I still couldn't tell if she was covering, especially since she seemed so close to tears.

Talya nodded. "I'm good. It's just that when Austin started paying attention to you, I got a little insecure. It seemed like maybe he was moving on."

"Look, I am not interested in Austin. So you don't have to worry about that." But as I said it, I felt a small pang of guilt, like I was lying to her.

"Good. Because I can't handle you stealing another guy from me." That stung. I started to get defensive but the look on Talya's face showed me she was feeling vulnerable and insecure about Austin. And about me. I also knew I had to let this one go. Brandon and I had finally moved on and revisiting last year wasn't going to do anyone any good. Still, I wasn't sure what to make of Talya's confession about her first time with Austin. I wanted to ask her more and make sure she wasn't covering for him if he'd pushed her further than she'd wanted to go.

"Talya. You sure you're really okay about last night? I mean, I know we're not super close, but—"

"I'm fine. Really. It's all good." She started to walk away but I didn't want to let it go that easily. I could tell she was bothered, between lying about who she had been with to not knowing what had really happened. I mean, who would be okay with a big black hole in her memory?

"Are you sure, because—?" I started.

"Yes. I'm sure," she said.

And she shut me down.

Jamie blew a whistle and waved a hand. She hadn't stopped moving since we'd gotten there, going from hauling out new piles of equipment to dropping platters of food on tables and leaning in for a few words of conversation, never putting down the mammoth sandwich she held in her fist. "Hey, y'all, anyone want to help with the dishes? Doing it now gets you out of KP at dinner. C'mon. I know, it's a real seductive offer. . . ." Talya raised her hand to volunteer and hopped up, apparently feeling better now that she'd gotten things off her chest.

"There we go. Thank you, Talya," Jamie said. "Now I just need two more victims, I mean, volunteers." A couple of other kids ambled over and I resigned myself to dinner dish duty.

Talya started gathering up the dishes off the various tables, occasionally casting a glance in Austin's direction. He avoided her gaze. Finally, she dropped what she was doing and went to where he was standing. They talked for a couple minutes, and at one point in the conversation, I realized they were both looking at me. And then I realized I'd been staring at the two of them. When Talya came back for KP duty, I decided to ask Austin what that was all about. But when I looked over, he was gone.

Chapter 14

Before we could settle into too much recreation and maybe believe we might have the afternoon off, Jamie had us hiking back up the hill with arms full of new supplies: ropes, boxes of wooden planks, and buckets of nails. I asked Jamie what everything was for, but she wouldn't tell me. "In due time. All will be revealed to you," she said, spreading her arms like a yogi.

Her magical mountain act wasn't instilling quite the level of anticipation she might have wanted for what was to come. I rolled my eyes and looked around the group, trying to spot Austin, as we trudged up the hill. I didn't want to make Talya feel any worse by spending more time with him, but I was worried about her, and if he was using her, I was gonna rip him a new one. But I didn't see him anywhere in the group. In fact, after he'd seen us talking together, he'd disappeared.

"Hey, a bunch of us were talking about later. We're sneaking down to the lake," Gracie said, coming up to walk with me.

"Though I'm not really sure it's sneaking since no one seems to care if we're out. You know Bryce bailed out after he thought he scared us with his reading of the rules last night. I think the whole curfew thing was just a ruse for the parents," Jaden said. Max was hanging in the back, talking to a couple of the other guys. I was tempted to talk to him about the whole Austin thing, but I didn't really think it deserved an audience.

Riley was walking next to Gracie, not participating in the conversation. I didn't know her that well, but it seemed like she'd been quiet all day. I realized the tension between Talya and Austin had me reading into everyone's behavior for no reason. Maybe the wilderness had a subduing effect on Riley or maybe there wasn't any reason for anything. I had to mellow out.

"You going to the lake?" I asked. She shrugged and looked at the mountain we were apparently about to climb.

"Depends on if I have any energy after scaling that thing," she said, pointing. I looked up. This was no mere hill like the one we'd walked up earlier in the day. This definitely qualified as a mountain.

"We're not going up there. There's no way they'd make us do that," I said, feeling certain. Then I looked at Jamie, who'd dropped her load of supplies at the bottom of a trail that snaked back and forth in about a million switchbacks up the mountain. "Seriously, Jamie. We're not hiking that hill. Some of us aren't jocks."

"Oh, you look like you're in plenty good shape to me," she said, sizing me up.

"No, you don't understand. I do whatever I can to avoid gym. To avoid any movement at all, actually."

My protests only got me my own personal load of ropes and a bucket of nails. "Well, then this'll be good for you, girlfriend. Consider it Pilates on a hill."

There was no use protesting where Jamie was concerned. She was scanning the group of us, waiting to see if anyone else was dumb enough to mouth off and earn an extra load to carry. "Come on, it's not a punishment. It's a challenge. Find your courage," she said, handing off a bucket of nails to Riley and splitting a pile of wood between Jaden and Max, who she led to a different area with Talya and a few others. I would have liked Max to be in our group. Making small talk with everyone else didn't thrill me.

It turned out that courage was needed not just for the hike up the giant mountain but for the job ahead of us: building a suspension bridge over a gap in the trail. The rain had worn away the dirt to the point that the trail dead-ended at what looked like a dry river bed. "Why do we need a bridge over this? Can't people just climb down and then go back up again?" I asked, demonstrating by jumping the four or so feet down into the gap.

"Sure, when it's dry," Jamie said. "But what do you think happens in a year when we aren't having a massive drought?" We all looked at her blankly. "I know you probably consider year-round beach weather a good thing, but believe it or not, it's actually supposed to rain. Sometimes it really does. And when that happens, this lake fills with water and no one can cross it to go further on the mountain."

"Sounds like nature's way to me," Jaden said. "Maybe no one's meant to cross it and climb up this huge thing."

Jamie smiled and handed him a few more pieces of wood. "Go. Build. Repeat. Make me proud."

And we were off. It turned out that building a suspension bridge was a kind of torture. Both mental and physical. Jaden and I measured out the rope and hammered stakes into the ground on the two riverbanks. Then we stretched the ropes across and pulled them taught. The harder part was nailing the boards to the ropes. And when I say ropes, I'm not talking about flimsy strings of twine. These had the circumference of a quarter, like the ropes used to tie a ship to a cleat on the shore. Nothing was chewing through these ropes. We nailed the boards on one after another until we'd built kind of a makeshift ladder going across the gap. I imagined walking across it and immediately felt something like seasickness mixed with outright fear.

"Okay, there's no way I'd walk across that, no offense," I said.

"Maybe if the alternative was an ice bath in a melted snowcap, you'd give it a try," Jaden said.

"No, I think we need to make it stronger."

We looked again at our supplies and couldn't figure out how a bunch of boards nailed to pieces of rope would ever be strong enough. That was when Jamie came over and told us we'd been doing the whole thing wrong. "You need ropes for your hands. To hold on to when you walk across. You attach them to stakes that you'll nail in every foot or so." She demonstrated, holding up the ropes and stakes and making the whole thing look logical to anyone other than a bunch of city kids who might as well have built the thing out of licorice for all the durability our version had.

"So how are we supposed to build this thing so it's stable?" Gracie asked.

"I want you to figure that out. Exciting, right?" Jamie said, winking and dropping the ropes and stakes to the ground. Of course that was what she wanted. She walked away like she'd just gifted us with the most important life skill ever. We went back to the pile of supplies and stared at them for a while, willing the bridge to build itself. When that didn't happen, we faced our fears and started laying out the ropes and wooden boards again, this time trying to look at everything in an exciting new light. Which was hard.

I looked up at the others. Gracie and Jaden shrugged, but Riley was nodding like this all made sense. "I get it. We need tension. That's how the whole thing is gonna hold together. It's just physics." She started laying the ropes out on the ground and positioning a second set to act as a handrail. Then she laid out the boards about a foot apart and put another set down for the base of the bridge. "See? If we have handrails nailed in, it will stabilize the whole thing, and give whoever's walking something to hold on to."

We all looked at her like she'd just turned a piece of string into a race car. But then it all made sense. Physics.

"Guess you earned your A the hard way," Jaden said.

"Damn right. She's seriously brilliant," Gracie said. Riley looked away at the compliment and I'm pretty sure she was blushing.

It didn't take us long to nail everything together once Riley had laid it all out for us. When Jamie came back, I could tell she was impressed. She looked at her watch, then at the sky, where the sun was still making a high arc over the trees. I hoped our reward for doing this right wasn't going to be another bridge to build or an even steeper hike. I guess I was glaring at her without realizing it. "Don't look at me like that," she told me. "I'm not evil. You earned yourselves the rest of the day free."

"Woo-hoo," Jaden yelled, and fist-bumped Riley.

Jamie headed to where Max and Talya were still suffering through a different kind of bridge. "Don't thank me too loudly or anything," she yelled as she walked away.

We looked down the trail ahead of us. Even though it was now in partial shade, it was still a long way to walk. "I think we earned a break before we do any more hiking, don't you guys?" I asked. I didn't have to convince anyone. My legs were aching from all the walking we'd been doing and all I could think about was curling up somewhere and taking a nap, like maybe if I willed it, a patch of cool grass would grow beneath my feet.

We found a spot under some trees and arranged our backpacks so we could sit on them and still have a rock or a tree to lean against. A part of me felt totally natural out there, like I could spend more time away from my regular life, but a much bigger part was completely relieved this was a temporary weekend thing. It was still dirt and rocks.

"Okay, who's up for a party later?" Gracie asked. "I still have some vodka from last night and a whole bag of gummy worms for chasers."

"I didn't just hear you say that," Max said, walking over with Talya, who giggled and brushed a hand on his arm. "Gummy worm hater?" I knew the look she was giving him. It was the same way she'd been staring at Austin the day before. So much for her love connection the previous night. Or maybe she was just flirting with everyone.

I knew I had no claim on Max, but it bugged the crap out of me that Talya was moving on to him. And that he was letting her. I tried to catch his eye to see if he thought she was as ridiculous in her flirting as I did, but he was beaming at her like she'd just invented the sun.

"Oh, he's just giving me a hard time because I can't do shots. I have to, like, drink them and then I need something massively sweet right afterward," Gracie said.

"She drinks like a girl," Jaden teased. Gracie threw a rock at him and almost hit him in the head. He smirked. "We used to date," he explained, still grinning at Gracie like he loved pushing her buttons.

She wasn't having any of it. "And I was awesome. But we were a disaster. Together, I mean. So now we just love each other as friends."

"With occasional benefits," Jaden added. Talya perked up at that. I couldn't tell if she was jealous or if she just didn't want to miss a bit of the gossip.

"TMI, people. Seriously, is that all you can talk about?" Riley sniped. Gracie looked at her in surprise.

"What's your problem? You've been acting weird all day."

"Nothing. I just don't think we need a list of every sex buddy you've ever had."

"Not even what I was saying," Gracie said, apparently annoyed but a little indifferent to the criticism.

"Oh, forget it. I guess I'm just tired," Riley said. She got up and walked to a patch of ground where there were pinecones, bending to examine them like she'd become completely absorbed in their wonder. Anything to get away from the conversation. Something was up.

"Well, I'm up for a party later," Talya said. "Is there alcohol?" She looked at me after she said it. I wasn't sure if it was a warning not to say anything about the previous night or if she was asking my permission to get drunk again.

"All right, a girl who wants to let loose," Jaden said. "Well, here's the sitch. We brought stuff for last night, but we didn't know how much we'd be able to get away with, so our stash is kind of dry. But I heard the director has booze in the staff bunk. Maybe we can steal it."

"Jamie? She seems so straight," Talya said. I had to agree. I couldn't imagine Jamie chugging down vodka after-hours.

"I meant Bryce, but I hear Jamie has her fun, too," Jaden said. It bothered me to hear him talking about her. I don't know why, but I felt protective.

"Who'd you hear that from?"

"Oh, I have my sources," he said, winking. "If you

come to the lake tonight, maybe I'll reveal them to you."
I shrugged like I'd consider it. I didn't want them to get
the impression I was no fun at all. Actually, I didn't want
them to have any impression of me. I really just wanted
to keep my head down and get through this weekend and
back to my life.

"Whatever. I don't need to know."

"Well, I do. Dish. What's Jamie into?" Gracie asked.

Jaden knew he had a live one in Gracie and he savored
the moment, pretending to zip his lips closed and throw
away the key. He knew that would drive her insane.

"C'mon. Tell. Unless you're full of it and you know
nothing," Gracie said.

"Just let it go. Why do you always have to look for
the worst in people? Jamie's entitled to her privacy," Riley
called from a few paces away. Gracie whipped her head
around and stared at Riley, both shocked and annoyed.
The rest of us were equally shocked. Riley and Gracie
were practically inseparable. They bantered like a married
couple who finished each other's sentences and knew
what the other one was thinking before she even had a
chance to realize it herself. But something was definitely
bugging Riley.

"Why are you acting like such a freak?" Gracie asked.
"Seriously, what crawled up your butt and died today?"

Riley glared at her and said nothing. Finally, she
shook her head. "You know what? I'm so done with all of

this." She didn't say more, and by the look on her face, Gracie didn't understand what she was talking about any more than I did.

Riley wasn't hanging around to provide details. She dropped the rope she'd been carrying and started marching down the trail, just shy of a full-on run. I looked at Gracie, expecting her to follow and get to the bottom of what was going on with her friend, but she stood there looking puzzled and finally shrugged. "Hormones are a bitch, right?" She didn't even make a move to follow Riley. Instead, she picked up the conversation where Jaden had left it. "Okay, so let's hear about Jamie."

I didn't stay to find out what Jaden had to say. "You know what, I'm gonna head back and hit the showers before everyone uses all the hot water." I picked up my backpack, which felt heavier than I remembered it from a few minutes earlier, and started walking down the trail. I could see Riley in the distance and I didn't exactly jog to catch up with her, but I thought if we had a few minutes alone at the site, I could maybe find out what was wrong.

I had her in my sights most of the walk down the trail. But when I got back to our bunk, she was nowhere to be found.

Chapter 15

By the time evening rolled around, Riley had rejoined the rest of us and seemed okay, so I didn't pull her aside and interrogate her. But it seemed like she was keeping her distance from Gracie, who didn't appear to notice or care. Instead, she'd turned her attention to Talya, who was getting ready for her night out by the lake like it was senior prom.

Talya dragged all of us to the bathroom to crowd in front of the tiny mirror and assess how she looked. We all gave her outfit a thumbs-up, but it would be hard to screw up a pair of jeans and a tight T-shirt with Yogi Bear on the front. She actually looked younger in that shirt, even though it emphasized every curve. Maybe it was

Yogi. Then she caught a glimpse of herself in the mirror and started groaning.

"Seriously, how is today the day my face decided to give me a big fat zit?"

"Maybe it's the mountain air," I said. "Weird environments can mess with your skin. Plus all the sweat and sunscreen." I checked out my own face in the mirror, curious to see if I looked any different after my day in the woods. So far, I hadn't transformed into anything but a dirtier version of myself.

"OMG, do I look hideous or what?" Talya whined.

"No one will even notice. It'll be dark," Gracie said. "Don't worry. Besides, it's nothing a little cover-up can't fix." She whipped open a makeup kit that rivaled half the cosmetics counters in Macy's. I couldn't believe the array of shades and shadows of eye makeup and blush and lip stain.

I looked at my own face again, completely naked of makeup, and couldn't decide if I liked the earthy me or if I was just rationalizing because I wouldn't even know what to do with half of those brushes and powders.

Riley hadn't said anything. She was watching Gracie give Talya a makeover, starting with a layer of powder foundation. "Look, see? Your skin's totally smooth now. You can't even see the zit." Talya looked at her reflection in the distorted metal and realized she just had to take Gracie's word for it. Gracie expertly brushed a layer of blush on Talya's cheeks and swept a few different shades of brown across her brow. She moved at warp speed, like someone who'd trained to apply makeup in a competition. Finally, she added the lip stain and a dot of gloss. I had to admit Talya looked really pretty. She hugged Gracie and turned to us. I nodded in approval, feeling a twinge of envy that Gracie had chosen Talya as her own personal Cinderella. Not that I wanted a makeover, and I'm sure Gracie would've jumped at the chance to turn me into a princess.

"I thought you looked pretty before," Riley said. She was kind that way and it wasn't just lip service. She looked past appearances and seemed to see what was really in a person. I wondered how she and Gracie had become such good friends when they seemed so completely different.

"Hey, Callie, can I borrow your brown belt? These jeans are falling off me." I looked and saw that her jeans weren't even covering half her thong underwear and her T-shirt was tiny. A rescue operation was needed, and fast.

"So tell me about Max. What's his deal?" I heard Talya ask Gracie as I walked away.

"Oh, he's a sweetie. Who's asking, Miss Thing?" Gracie said. I felt myself sigh. Why did I care, really, who Talya stalked for her next conquest? I thought about seeing Brandon in a couple of hours and felt calmed by that feeling of comfortable relief.

The sun had all but disappeared in the time we'd

spent watching Talya transform herself into a goddess of the trails, and the dusky sky had turned everything a royal shade of blue. I couldn't remember if I'd ever seen this color at home. It was the same sky, the same sun. Maybe I'd just never looked before. Or maybe the mountain air did change things.

It was getting darker every minute, and by the time I reached our tent, I knew I'd need a flashlight to make my way back. I guess I left the door open while I searched around on my bed for wherever I'd left the flashlight the night before. It had fallen in the crack behind the bed and I had my face practically stuffed into a pillow reaching for it. So I didn't hear Austin come in behind me.

"Hey." I must've jumped, because he started to laugh. "Whoa, didn't mean to scare you." I backed slowly out from under the top bunk, making sure not to whack my head as I stood and looked at him. He was hovering in the doorway, leaning on it, and looking at me in that lazy way that made him look like he'd just had the best sex ever and was basking in its glow.

"Hi," I said. I didn't know where to begin. After he'd kind of let his guard down earlier, I thought maybe he'd tell me the truth about Talya, but she was acting so weird, like she was totally over it. I didn't know where to begin.

"You're mad." He pushed himself away from the door frame but had trouble standing straight. He wove from side to side like he was drunk.

"I'm . . . I don't know what I am."

He smiled and took a step toward me. "I do. . . . You're adorable."

I felt a flutter of warmth when he spoke and I was furious at my body for feeling anything at all toward him. Anything but annoyance and possibly hate.

"Get drunk much?" I asked. "Or really, I should say, get other people drunk and take advantage of them? Is that why you're here knocking on my door?" There. I said it. Now it was his turn to do some talking.

"I don't think I knocked. I just came in."

"You should go."

"I don't wanna go." He came in and sat on Talya's bed. I wondered if he had any idea it was hers. "I can't stop thinking about you."

He was good at this. He had a way of seeming like he was pouring his heart out, opening up and making himself vulnerable. In my heart I knew he was just playing his game, telling me what he thought I wanted to hear. But if you wanted to believe him, if you needed to hear someone telling you you rocked his world—like Talya seemed to need—he would be hard to resist.

I'd been burned by guys like him, guys who'll say anything because they're so good at knowing what you need to hear. I used to be more desperate to believe what other people were willing to tell me, usually to get something in return. I like to think I'm a little smarter now.

135

"Will you come out with me? C'mon, everyone's going down to the lake. We could go somewhere else. . . ."

"Weren't you just with Talya last night? What, is it like a new-girl-every-night kind of thing for you?"

He blinked slowly. Then he took a flask out of his pocket and unscrewed the metal cap. He offered it to me before taking a drink himself. I was tempted, but I was also still on probation and I had a feeling getting caught drinking was not the life experience Lena and Stef imagined for me this weekend. "No thanks."

"Is that like 'no thanks, I don't drink'? Or 'no thanks, I wouldn't get caught dead drinking with you'?" I didn't answer. Seemed like he knew. He took a drink from the flask and screwed the cap back on.

Just to mess with whatever impression he had of me, I reached for the flask and took a swig. It tasted awful, warm rotgut tequila. I don't even know why I did it. It wasn't enough to have much of an effect on me, but I did feel the heat of the alcohol roll through my insides. It just made me feel worse.

"I get that it's hard for you, with Tals. I just want you to know that."

"What's hard?"

He shrugged. "I guess I just figure it brings up old issues." I mean, he was drunk, sure, but none of this made sense.

"I'm not sure what you think you know, but—"

136

"That you and your brother were doing the nasty," he said, watching my face for a reaction. I did my best to control my expression but not before I flinched slightly. He noticed.

"Every time you have the chance at being a good guy," I said. I looked him right in the eye, determined not to let him intimidate me.

"So it's true." He pumped a fist in the air, like it was a personal victory for him to confirm his suspicions. "Man, it's hard to get information out of you. You're the type who's always wary and shut down. Me, I'm just trying to get to know you better." And, of course, Talya had helped him out there. She was using this weekend to stick it to me, first by smearing my secrets all over the place and then by going after Max. I felt a flush working its way across my cheeks.

"What exactly are you hoping to gain here?" I could feel the flush building, and the best thing I could do was abort this conversation and walk away, but part of me needed to know who he'd been talking to.

He smirked, working some angle I hadn't figured out yet. "I'm just having a conversation."

"Yeah, well, conversation's over." I had found the flashlight and now I had to look around for the brown belt Talya wanted. I opened my duffel bag and could feel Austin's eyes on me while I searched.

"Wow, are you giving me the cold shoulder? I was just

telling you I get it. There's no judgment." I didn't answer. "Look, if you want to keep your deep, dark secrets to yourself, I'm cool with that. Just tell me to back off."

"Okay. Back off." I found the belt and rolled it up. It fit in my pocket and I looked around the room to see if there was anything else I should grab before heading out. I'd leave Austin in our room if I had to. But I was getting out of there.

He didn't need to be told twice. He stood up and made his way unsteadily toward the door. "You're no fun, Callie. I thought you were fun, but you're not," he slurred.

I thought about whether to let things go, as pissed as I was at Talya. She seemed okay with everything, and she certainly wasn't running around worried about my feelings. But the big sister in me felt like I wanted to protect her, even if she didn't deserve it. "The thing with Talya last night?" I said. He turned, looking bored with the conversation.

"Yeah?"

"Did you know how drunk she was? I mean, did she seem like she knew what she was doing?"

"Aw, is that what you're worried about? Not a prob. Your girl Tals was just fine. We did most of our drinking afterward. It was all good." He wasn't gloating. He didn't look like some self-satisfied he-man. He was just conveying information.

I was sorry I'd gotten involved. It wasn't like Talya had

been honest about anything that weekend, so I shouldn't have been surprised to hear two different versions of the story from her and Austin. Still, she seemed vulnerable, really needing to believe he liked her.

"But do you . . . you know, are you into her? Really?"

He smiled and shook his head. "You just don't get it, do you? I noticed you the second you got on the bus. You're the one I can't stop thinking about. That's why I wanted to know about your past. I want to know you. So no, I'm not into your friend. She was a nice diversion and we had some fun. But no. I want you. Totally."

He suddenly seemed very serious and dead sober. His eyes were boring into mine and I couldn't stop my heart from pounding. Did I want him, too? Did it matter? Nothing was going to happen with anyone on this trip. I needed to remind myself of that, one more time. This was not the right time to even consider believing that Austin meant what he was saying.

"I have to go," I said. "People are waiting for me." I started to edge past him, willing myself not to feel anything toward him as I passed just inches away.

"You're breaking my heart," he said. He wasn't pleading. More just stating it as fact. Then he turned to go. It took a moment, but then I remembered to breathe again.

Chapter 16

From our bunk, I could hear raucous laughter in the direction of the lake and I assumed Bryce and Jamie heard the clear signs of partying, too. Their building wasn't too far from ours, but maybe they were out doing something on their own. At the very least, their warnings about not breaking curfew seemed to be pretty meaningless. Maybe it was designed to scare us into submission.

Talya and Gracie were already at the lake and Riley hung back with Jaden, who was eliciting her help in drawing up an elaborate plan to sneak into Bryce's office and grab some gin or rum or whatever he kept hidden there according to Jaden's "sources." It was strange that Gracie didn't seem bothered by Riley's mood, or if she was, she pretended not to be. I knew from experience that sometimes it's better to leave a person alone and let her figure it out on her own. When Jude had stopped talking for a while, everyone being in his face trying to get him to feel better just put more pressure on him. When we finally backed off and he felt like I understood what he needed, it had done the trick. So I decided to let Riley and Gracie work it out, at least for now.

"Hey, Callie, you want to help us on our alcohol grab? We could use an extra lookout," Jaden said, peeking into our bunk.

"Yeah, come on, Callie! Less of a chance of getting busted if we're all in it together," Riley yelled from outside.

I came out. She was wearing all black. "You look like a cat burglar," I said, laughing.

"In the dark, no one will be able to see me."

"I understand why you did the clothes, but it just seems a little extreme. If no one's there, no one will be around to catch you. And if someone's in the room, all the black clothes in the world aren't really gonna hide you."

"I know that. Wow, you're even more logical than me and I'm about as up in my head as they come," she said, but then she smiled. I considered using this as a way in to talk about what seemed to be bugging her, but it felt weird with Jaden there.

Jaden looked her over and laughed. "Awesome, now I've got two brainy partners in crime." It was maybe the first time anyone had called me brainy, but I wasn't about to correct him.

I was conscious of the time. I didn't want to be late meeting Brandon, but I didn't want to tell them that. And I didn't want to use the same excuse as last night about being tired and staying in the bunk, so I figured I could spend a few minutes trying to help them out. "Okay, what's the plan? I'm not wearing a catsuit, but I'll help."

"Well, I checked out the doors to the office earlier, and like everything here, they're practically made of tinfoil. So I should be able to pick the lock with a paper clip." He pulled one out of his pocket and showed me that he'd already straightened it on one side so he could insert it into the lock.

"How're you gonna know no one's in there?" I asked.

"Simple. We'll knock, and if someone answers, we'll just use some excuse about needing to borrow a couple blankets."

"We were supposed to bring our own blankets," I reminded him.

"Or whatever. We'll come up with something," Jaden said, wanting to get on with it.

"I'm just saying, you should have a more convincing story. No reason to be scrambling on the spot to come up with something believable."

143

"You think like a thief," Riley said. Then I could tell she immediately felt bad, because she actually took a step back and started stammering. "I didn't mean . . . cause you were in jail . . . I wasn't saying—"

"I know you weren't. Don't worry," I told her. But it was kind of true. I don't know why my mind worked the way it did. Either it was because I'd gotten good at making up excuses for things I wasn't supposed to be doing or maybe I was just a good liar by nature. But this wasn't like running away from home. It didn't require a crazy amount of planning, just a convincing excuse. "Why don't you just say you wanted to know if there was any more dessert?" I said.

"Fine, we'll use that," Jaden said. "But anyway, shouldn't be too hard. If no one answers, we'll sneak in and grab whatever we can."

"Aren't you worried they'll miss it?" I asked, my criminal brain at work again.

Jaden shook his head and held up a backpack filled with bottles. Some were empty and some had water in them. "We'll put whatever we take in these bottles," he said, indicating the empties. "And replace whatever alcohol we steal with water. By the time they figure it out, we'll be long gone from this retreat."

Sounded convincing enough. And not particularly dangerous. "Okay, but how is this a three-person job?" It wasn't exactly *Mission: Impossible*. I was feeling jittery about my own plans to sneak out and I wouldn't have minded sitting out this particular caper.

"We need someone to stand guard at the front and one at the back while one of us goes inside. That way we'll have plenty of warning if someone's coming."

I shrugged. Sounded like a simple enough plan. We made our way down the path to the office without passing anyone. A good sign because no one would even be able to say they saw us there. Jaden knocked and waited. No answer.

"Better knock again, just to be sure," I said. I didn't know how big the office was. What if someone was in another part of the building? He knocked again and waited. Still nothing.

None of us said anything. Jaden slipped the paper clip into the lock and it clicked. The door inched open a tiny bit and we peeked in. No one anywhere in sight. Jaden pointed me to the back side of the building and Riley stepped back to keep watch from the front.

No sooner had I gone out to keep watch than I saw Bryce walking up the path. We hadn't really talked about what, exactly, we were supposed to do if someone came. I hurried around to the front to let Riley know Bryce was coming so she could warn Jaden, but I didn't see her anywhere. Crap. I went back around and practically ran into Bryce. He was a fast walker.

"Whoa," he said. "Slow down. Everything okay?" I

tried to wipe the look of panic off my face but I could tell I'd failed because his expression instantly turned dire. "What's wrong? Is someone hurt?"

"Oh, no, nothing like that. Everything's fine. I just . . . wanted to know if there was any more . . . dessert." When I heard the words, I realized how thin my manufactured excuse sounded. I wished we'd spent a little more time coming up with something better. I heard what sounded like chairs scraping on the floor and then some shuffling of something heavy coming from the office. I looked again at Bryce to see if he'd heard it and sensed that something was up.

"Hold on," he said. He went around to the front of the office. Clearly he'd heard the noises. Who wouldn't? It sounded like Jaden was training a team of stuntmen in there. I followed close behind, worried for Jaden and Riley and also for myself. If I got myself in trouble now, there was no way I'd be able to sneak out and meet Brandon. As soon as we rounded the corner, I saw Riley and Jaden sitting on a rock near the office. "Oh, hey, man," Jaden said to Bryce. "Awesome sunset, isn't it? We just caught it before it dipped." Riley pointed out across the meadow where the sun was perfectly perched at the top of the hill. "Look, perfect timing."

The two of them were acting so casual they actually made me believe they'd been sitting there forever, not ransacking the office moments before. "Yup, it's like this every day in the summer," Bryce said. "Pretty gorgeous, right?"

"Guys, I'm heading back to camp. Wanna join?" I asked, still feeling my heart racing in my chest. They got up casually and we wandered down the path, none of us speaking until we'd gone a fair distance. Then Jaden cracked up.

"That was classic. He totally bought it."

"Did you get the stuff?" I asked. Jaden unzipped his backpack and showed me the full bottles, enough to get a football team and a half completely plastered. "C'mon," he said. "Let's head down to the lake."

I had to make it seem like I was hanging out with everyone else. If lots of people could say they saw me down by the lake it would be a lot easier to sneak out and not be missed. People would assume I'd walked back to my bunk. Or over to the bathrooms. Then I'd turn up later at the lake and no one would be the wiser. At least that was my plan.

I followed Jaden and Riley down the path that led to the lake. We rounded a corner and I could see the yellow reflection of the sun on the still evening water. From where we stood, the hills no longer obstructed the path of the sun, and it had sunk down halfway below the horizon. It looked like a half-moon of light sitting on the lake, getting smaller by the minute, until it faded out like a dollop of melting butter. The party was in full swing even without Jaden's pack of stolen vodka, but when we showed up, everyone gravitated toward Jaden, empty cups ready.

I heard a familiar voice behind a nearby clump of trees. "I couldn't stop thinking about you." Austin. I turned, wary of him trying to charm me again, when I saw that he wasn't alone. Talya had a mile-wide smile on her face and started giggling when he stroked her arm.

"That tickles," she squealed. "But don't stop."

"I don't wanna stop," he said, leaning in to kiss her. I suddenly felt like a creepy stalker and backed away quickly before they spotted me. I couldn't believe him. An hour earlier he'd used the exact same line on me and I'd fallen for it, seriously thinking he meant what he said. I wondered what had become of Max. Had Talya already dumped him or had he moved on instead? I decided I didn't really care.

Everyone else had filled their cups and a small group was wading through the shallow water at the shore toward a large flat rock, cups held high.

"Hey," Riley yelled, and Gracie waved her over. Riley waded out to follow her and I took my cue to retrace my steps quietly down the path and out of sight.

I waited in our bunk for the sky to get dark and made sure I had my flashlight so I could see on the road once I snuck out of camp. Then I carefully moved past the office and down the service road, which got darker by the minute. I could feel mosquitoes sniping at my face but I couldn't see them. I felt the ice-cold of metal at my outstretched fingertips just seconds before I was up against the chain-link fence. A harrowing climb in total blackness, and I was free.

Chapter 17

It was dark on the road. Really dark. Jamie had remarked on it earlier and talked like it was a good thing, the complete stillness of the dark. She knew she had a bunch of city kids on her hands and she could have done a real number on us with ghost stories about limbless spooks and rabid animals hunting in the night. Instead she talked about how the quiet of the wilderness made her feel safe. The chances of anything bad happening out here were microscopic compared to the trouble we could get into in a city full of people, but I could tell none of us felt convinced that the cold, chilly darkness was the safe haven Jamie was describing. Especially now, when there was no safety in numbers and only my overactive brain hearing things that probably weren't really ravenous, wild pack animals in the distance.

I was afraid to turn on my flashlight in case somehow the road was visible from camp. The paranoia from almost getting caught by Bryce stayed with me, and I felt an extra layer of anxiety about being out here alone. Why did I need to sneak out so badly? I thought about the little voice living inside me that pushed me to make reckless decisions. I couldn't remember whether I had always been this way. I couldn't remember a time when I hadn't.

The air had really cooled down when the sun had dropped earlier, and I could have really used another layer. I was pretty sure I'd be able to see my breath in front of me when I exhaled if I could see anything at all. I wasn't sure how Brandon was going to find me in the complete blackness. Unless his high beams washed over me, he could just as easily drive right past me and never know I was out there. So I crept out of the shadowy shoulder of the lane and walked in the road, which made me feel pretty vulnerable to being sideswiped by a passing car, even if I did have the warning of headlights bearing down.

I decided to switch on my flashlight but keep it pointed at the ground, at least to light the path in front of me and give passing cars a fighting chance of not running me over. Right about now I was regretting mocking Stef's headlamp that she'd tried to loan me for the weekend. "I'm not going into a coal mine," I'd said.

"You'll thank me for this, I promise. You just pop it on and you're hands free. And you can see wherever your head is pointed." She'd demonstrated by pulling the strap around her head and turning it on, looking all around her bedroom and finally leveling a stare at me. "This is an interrogation. You will tell me all."

I laughed. "Do you do that at work? Shine it in people's eyes to get them to tell you stuff?"

"Never tried it before, but it's not a bad idea," she said. "No, I've actually had this for years. When I was pregnant with Brandon, I had the worst bout of insomnia and Mike was always pulling double shifts back then. So I'd put this thing on and read so I wouldn't wake him."

The image of Stef in her headlamp made me miss home even more. I looked down the road in both directions, willing my eyes to pick out the sign of headlights in the distance. For a second, I thought I saw something and I felt my heart jump with nervous anticipation mixed with fear of getting caught. But it turned out to be a tiny swarm of fireflies, which I might have found interesting since I'd never actually seen a real firefly before, but instead I just felt annoyed.

The whole no-cell-phones thing was making this much harder. I was actually forced to use the sun as my gauge of time. I knew the sunset was at around seven, and I tried to calculate the time I'd spent with Riley and Jaden and the time I'd spent by the lake. That was at least an hour. Plus, I'd been walking for what seemed like forever, but was probably at least another half hour. Or maybe more? We'd planned to meet at 8:30. What was taking him so long?

I stopped walking, not wanting to get too far away from camp. Brandon would drive me back, of course, but for the first time since coming up with my genius plan to sneak out, I realized how insanely dumb it was. What if I got lost? Or abducted by some crazy trucker who knew these roads much better than I did? This was not a good plan. And Brandon was late. Or maybe he wasn't coming at all. In my mind, I replayed the moments before I'd left for this place. He'd said he would come. Hadn't he? Maybe he'd never intended to meet me and I had idiotically scaled a fence thinking we had a deal.

I backed away from the road and leaned against a tree. My eyes had adjusted and there was a sliver of moon in the sky now. I could see my own feet without the flashlight, which made me feel slightly better.

And then I saw it: a beam of light coming down the road. I hadn't paid much attention when the bus had taken us up there, so I didn't know whether we'd come from the direction of the lights or the road behind me. Either way, it was a sign of humanity. Or a crazy trucker.

The light was getting closer, but now I could see that

it was just a single beam, and it wasn't shining steadily like the headlights of a car. It was bouncing around.

Like someone on foot. With a flashlight. Someone from camp.

I was so busted.

Chapter 18

I had only moments to decide what to do before the person with the flashlight was on me. *Relax,* I told myself. Maybe it was just Jamie out for a walk, looking to commune with nature. And I was practically invisible where I stood. *Just sit tight and maybe you'll get away with this,* I thought.

"Callie," I heard a voice call. But it wasn't Jamie. It was a male voice, for one thing. For a second I thought maybe it was Brandon. Maybe he'd parked up the road and come to find me on foot. "Are you okay?" I heard the voice say. But it wasn't his voice, even though my ear was trying to bend it into Brandon's. Still, it was a tiny bit familiar. And a second later, I knew why.

Max.

"Callie," he said when he got close, shining his flashlight on me. There was no getting out of this now. "What are you doing?"

"You followed me?" I was slightly glad to see him, only because my fears had started getting the better of me out there and there was safety in numbers. But I didn't appreciate being tracked like the fugitive I knew I was. "I don't remember telling you I wanted a sidekick." I knew it sounded bitter, but I couldn't help it. My annoyance with Talya spilling my life out to Austin, and his pouring out his heart to me one minute and making out with Talya the next, and Brandon's apparent no-show reared up in an explosion of annoyance. Max was just the closest thing to the flying shrapnel.

He turned off his flashlight and leaned against his own tree right next to mine. "Look, if you're done with me, just say so." He sighed. It was a strange choice of words.

"What do you mean, done with you? Do you think I just use people and toss them aside or something?" It felt good to take my anger out on someone, though I knew he was the wrong person. I couldn't help it. After this weekend, I'd probably never see him again, so what did it matter if he hated me?

"Maybe I should go."

"Fine by me," I said, planting my feet by the tree with

no idea what my own plan was. Part of me wanted to keep walking, to jeopardize this whole stupid trip and my grades at school. I felt exhausted. Exhausted from lugging rocks and ropes and exhausted from being angry at everyone.

"Callie . . ." He turned to look at me. The moon had risen even higher and I felt like it was shining right down on us. I could see his face and he looked anguished. "I don't know what's going on with you. Maybe I should, but I don't know you that well. I want to, though. Know you better."

I couldn't help it. Once I'd opened the floodgate to feeling angry, I couldn't hold back. It felt good to lash out, even at the wrong person. I wanted to keep going until I had nothing left. "Come on, at least come up with something less predictable. I'm sure it worked on Talya. But give me some credit." Why did I think I was better than Talya? The truth was I wanted to hear that I was special. And I couldn't stand that people could say those words and not mean them.

"Wow," was all Max said. But he didn't leave. I have no idea why. Why would anyone put up with me being a complete bitch and stick around? I realized I was trying to make him go, just so I could be alone again and feel sorry for myself.

So it caught me by surprise when he reached over and put his hand on my face. He held it there a moment and came closer, searching for something. A sign, maybe. Then he leaned in and kissed me. He wasn't tentative. It was a good kiss. Only it wasn't him trying to score. It was him trying to connect. I could tell the difference.

When he pulled away, he shook his head. "I know. You told me you're not open to anything. I just—"

I nodded, anger and frustration slipping away. That kiss melted me. I looked at him long and hard, trying to discern something in his face to let me know whether I could let my guard down. The truth was it was me I didn't trust anymore. I didn't trust myself to read people and know if they were likely to turn on me later on. I'd made some bad calls in the past and the bottom line was Austin had messed with my mind. And I'd let him. Just because he was a charmer and had that bad-boy/good-in-bed vibe, I'd let my guard down.

I wanted to believe Max. Not just because I needed to feel like someone was actually trustworthy, but because I needed to be able to trust my own instincts. I couldn't take it if my gut kept leading me astray. I had to be able to rely on it.

It was almost like he knew. "Callie . . . If you tell me you're not into this, I'm still here as a friend. You can trust me. Really. I'm not out for a onetime score."

I nodded. "I know." And I did. Max was one of the good guys. My gut told me so.

Max gave me another minute to maybe see if I might

160

come around and kiss him back. But I just couldn't. Then he flipped his flashlight on and shone it down the road. "We really should get back."

It occurred to me then that I didn't know why he was there. "Wait, did you follow me here?"

"Yeah."

"Why?"

He shrugged. "I knew something was up. You'd been avoiding me since Talya started hanging all over me earlier and I was coming to talk to you. But then I saw you heading down the service road and ripping out of camp like a bronco. Well, a sloppy bronco. You scale fences much?"

I had to laugh. It was dark out there, but even in the dimmest light I would have been quite a sight trying to get up and over the fence. "Nah, not since I broke out of juvie. Kidding."

"Anyway, I thought about just turning around and minding my own business." He shrugged. "I just followed you to make sure you were okay. I didn't want you to do anything stupid and get kicked out of here. Don't think that would go over well with your PO, right?"

"I wasn't planning on getting caught."

"Best laid plans . . ." he said. Then he started walking in the direction of camp. I looked down the road in both directions, straining my eyes for signs of Brandon, but all I could see was Max's flashlight bouncing along, friendly

161

like a firefly. I had no idea why Brandon hadn't shown up, but I'd have to deal with that later. For now, I jogged to catch up with Max. My friend Max.

Chapter 19

I opened the door to our bunk, expecting to be the first one back. Instead I heard a shriek. "Where were you?" Talya was splayed out on her bed, drunk as hell and over the moon. "I've been dying to talk to you for, like, hours."

I hadn't been gone for hours, but whatever. "What's up?" I hadn't stepped into the room yet. I actually was just stopping to grab a sweater before heading down to the lake, not just to bolster my alibi but because Max and I were going to hang.

I debated walking right out in the other direction and leaving Talya to bounce off the walls by herself, figuring her story could wait until later or she'd forget she even asked me to talk.

163

"OMG, I had the best night. With Austin." Of course, I knew she was with Austin but I didn't really want to hear a full recount of every moan and make-out moment.

"Talya, you know what? I'm heading out. Can we talk later?" I wasn't trying to blow her off, but I just wanted to have a little bit of fun and that didn't include being Talya's conscience and sounding board. And just being around her reminded me she'd blurted out my secrets to Austin and who knows who else.

"Aw," she said, making a pouty face and rolling onto her stomach, putting her chin in her hands. "Can't you stay a little bit?"

Ugh. I should have just walked away, but on our long walk back, Max and I had talked about why I felt so betrayed by Talya. He helped me put it in perspective. And I came out feeling more magnanimous toward her, despite myself. "Maybe a minute. What's up?"

She rolled from side to side, giggling. "Austin said he really wants a relationship. I'm so into him. I just wanted to tell you, 'cause you know, we're, like, friends now." I couldn't believe she didn't see it. I mean, Austin was the worst kind of jerk, the kind who'll say anything to get a girl in bed. If Talya didn't know that, I should tell her, right?

"Talya . . . the thing is . . . are you sure you believe what he's saying?"

She sat up, suddenly looking concerned. "Why wouldn't I?"

"Because he said the same thing to me not an hour before he was making out with you. It's just . . . I don't think . . . he's not a good guy." There. I couldn't help it. She had to know.

But my honesty didn't have the intended effect. Talya didn't turn to me and thank me for steering her clear of a dangerous guy.

"You're a bitch," she said, glaring at me. "Why are you doing this?"

"I'm not doing anything. I'm just telling you what I know." It's not like I was clueless. Of course she would assume I was trying to sabotage her chance at true love.

"Well, just . . . don't, okay?" She got up and started rifling through her bag. "Is this 'cause you're, like, jealous or something?"

Of course she'd think that. "No," I said quietly. "I promise you, I'm not jealous. I just . . . I've gotten to know him and I don't really trust him."

"Is this 'cause of what I told him about you and Brandon? He said you were bumming hard about that." She shook her head and dismissed it with a wave of her hand. "That's just his thing. He likes to know about people. Besides, I only told him stuff I thought was public knowledge."

She didn't see what was wrong with it, even now.

"You know what, Talya? I take it back. You and Austin are perfect for each other," I said. Then I shut the door and went down to the lake.

Chapter 20

I slept like a rock. Maybe it was because I'd carried so many of them, but my body hit the sagging springs of my bed and I fell into a deep, dark sleep that didn't end until the sun came streaming through the cracks in the blinds.

It took me a few minutes to recognize my surroundings. Then the memories of the night before came rushing in. First of all, let me say that my nature-guru powers of reading the sun and moon for an idea of the time were completely off. When Max and I snuck back into camp, we ran smack into Jamie and panicked that we were busted. But she didn't seem to suspect a thing. If anything, she seemed a little out of it and as soon as we got within range of her, I knew why. She reeked of pot. Maybe her dreadlocks had a superabsorbent sponge effect because Max and I looked at each other to confirm what we both smelled.

"Hey, all," she said. "You out for a walk before curfew? Good for you." She kept on moving, seeming like she didn't want to spend too much time with us. But I noticed the glow of her wristwatch and saw that it was only 8:45. Factoring the time it took us to walk back, I realized I must have left before Brandon ever had a chance to roll up and look for me. I felt terrible and wanted to go back to find him, but Max wouldn't budge. "You can't, Callie. There's no way you'd get past Jamie now." I knew he was right, but my heart still ached when it sunk in that I'd missed my chance for a family connection. Max put his arm around me, seeming to sense what I was thinking. And I realized I had the closest thing I'd have to a family connection right there.

We spent a couple of hours down by the lake, just hanging with everyone. Talya was a no-show, which was just as well, but Gracie and Jaden were pretty wasted and had stripped down to go skinny-dipping. "C'mon, you lame-os," Jaden said. "We're way ahead of you. Grab a drink and get your asses over here."

Let's just say my common sense got the better of me and I did not take off my clothes—at least not all of them—but I did do a cannonball off a rock into the freezing lake and didn't stop shivering until I climbed into bed later that night.

Lying in bed that morning I felt warm and comfortable, but the thought of getting up and building more bridges had a different effect. I turned over and saw that Talya and Gracie had both already left. Their beds, which I could see from mine, were empty and unmade. There was a smear of pink lipstick on Talya's pillow and her clothes from last night were strewn on the floor by her bed. Considering how dirty the floor was, I knew she'd been as drunk as she'd seemed when we'd talked. I felt relieved not to have another confrontation with her. At least not yet.

I moaned when I rolled over, assuming I was alone in the room. "Hey, you're up," Riley said. Startled, I scrambled out of bed and peeked over the rail to the top bunk of Riley's bed, where she was sitting up reading a mystery.

"Oh, I didn't think anyone was here." I felt groggier than usual. But also achy. Maybe it was the eighteenth jump off that rock. My head felt like it weighed eleven pounds. "Wow, my head feels like a block of cement."

"Drink much?" Riley swung her legs over the side of the bed and jumped down.

"I didn't drink at all, actually, but it sure feels like I did."

"Are you, like, on the wagon or something?" she asked. I didn't think people actually used that expression.

I shook my head "No. Just, you know, probation and stuff. I kind of have to stay on the straight and narrow."

"Right. I, um, didn't mean to . . . I don't know. I always say the wrong thing." She looked at the ground. Something had definitely changed since we'd gotten on the bus Friday night and I still couldn't figure out what it was. Riley threw a pink T-shirt on and grabbed her toothbrush.

"I'm coming with," I said. I followed her to the bathroom with my own toiletry bag. She didn't say anything. I waited until we were inside the bathroom and then checked under the stalls to make sure we were alone. "Hey, I know we don't know each other that well, but—"

Riley spun around to face me, her expression suddenly accusatory. "What?" she said impatiently. "What is it?"

I debated just aborting the whole conversation. She didn't seem open to talking and the last thing I needed at that point on the trip was one more confrontation. But I decided to go with my gut, which told me she needed someone to open up to. And in doing it, I knew I was taking a gamble on whether my gut had restored itself to trustworthy status. "Are you okay?" I'd planned to say more, or at least I was prepared to work harder to draw information out of Riley, after making her believe she could trust me. But after a moment of consideration, she burst into tears. I waited a moment to let her have some space, then walked over and gently put an arm around her. She clung to me and cried for a few minutes, not taking a break to speak.

When she'd gotten some of it out of her system, Riley backed away and went to the sink, washed off her face and began expertly applying makeup to cover the tracks of her outburst. "Sorry," was all she said.

"Do you, like, wanna talk about it?" I still wasn't sure of my role there, so I just hung back, figuring she'd tell me when she was ready. Meanwhile, I caught a glimpse of myself in the so-called mirror and practically jumped out of my skin at the witch staring back at me. My hair was tangled up in a ball with the hairband hanging in half a pigtail and my face looked red and squished on one side where I'd slept. Riley caught me looking and started to laugh despite herself. "I know, right?" I said. I pulled the rubber band out and tried to straighten my hair into something resembling normal.

We stared into the mirror in silence for a few minutes. I could hear some of the others coming back from breakfast, which I guessed we'd both missed by oversleeping. Finally, Riley turned to me and dished. "I have it bad for someone, okay? You know how it is when you just have all these . . . feelings and you're not sure the other person feels the same way, or maybe you're pretty sure they don't feel the same way . . . ?"

It all made perfect sense. The way she'd gotten upset

when Gracie talked about hooking up with Jaden, the way she'd gone from being super tight with Gracie to watching her from a distance. I wondered if Gracie knew Riley was pining for Jaden. "So does Gracie know?" I asked.

Riley looked embarrassed. "No. I don't really know how to tell her."

"Just be honest with her. You've been friends for, like, years, right? Friends tell each other stuff like this."

Riley didn't look so sure. "It's just . . . what if it ruins our friendship? I'm pretty sure she doesn't feel the same way."

I was confused. "She?"

"Gracie," she said, then looked at me like I'd taken a mental leave. "Are we having the same conversation?" I realized that up until that point, we hadn't been. Riley was in love with her best friend. I nodded, reassuring her I absolutely understood what we were talking about. "It's why when I heard you had two moms, I thought . . . but then I decided to keep it to myself."

Now that comment made sense, too. "Maybe Gracie kind of already knows. People sometimes do."

She looked at herself in the mirror while she talked to me. "She doesn't know. The only person I told is Max. He and I used to date." It surprised me that Max hadn't mentioned they'd been a couple. But it's not like we told each other everything there was to know in just two days. "When I came out to him, he was really great."

172

I shook the water from my toothbrush. I'd already straightened my hair and washed my face. I didn't have anything left to do in the bathroom but I didn't feel like I should leave, so I leaned against one of the stall doors.

"I could see him being like that," I said.

"So you think I should tell Gracie? I mean, there's a chance she feels the same way, right?" Her eyes looked pleadingly at me, wanting to believe she might have a chance with Gracie. I didn't want to disappoint her but Gracie didn't seem at all interested in girls.

Just then the door flew open and Jamie looked inside. "I was looking for you two. Come on, time to hit the trails. We're behind schedule already." She waited for us to exit the bathroom. We started to gather our things. "Forget about that stuff. No one's gonna take it. But we've gotta go. We've got two bridges to finish before lunch." There was no more time to finish our conversation. I took one last look in the mirror, pulled my hair into a ponytail, and followed Riley out.

Chapter 21

We spent half the morning building another two suspension bridges, but the time passed much more quickly than it had the day before. We'd gotten the hang of how to string the ropes over the wood to make hammering in the nails much easier. Riley, Max, and I got two bridges hung over the creek in the time it took to build one the day before. Riley was quiet but she seemed like a load had been lifted. She worked quickly with a smile on her face, resolved in the idea that she would tell Gracie how she felt later on. I wasn't sure we'd really come to that resolution in the bathroom, but I'd given her some space to feel it out.

"Hey, I've been thinking about what you said, you know . . . about telling?" I said.

Max shot me a warning look. *You're gonna talk about this now where anyone could overhear you?* But I looked around and there wasn't anyone nearby. It didn't matter. Max had a definite opinion on the situation. "Are you really prepared to have everything out in the open?" he asked Riley.

"You mean, am I ready to come out?" Riley asked. She sighed. Max put an arm around her but didn't say anything. I looked around again to see if anyone had come within hearing range. I started to think maybe Riley and Max should sort out whatever they had going on by themselves. But I couldn't see anyone and it felt weird to just start walking away for no reason.

"There are two parts to this," Max said. "There's the coming out part and the part where you tell Gracie you're in love with her. They're both huge."

He was right. It was one thing to let all the kids at school know you're gay. But I still couldn't help thinking there was more to Max's desire to have Riley keep this to herself than he was letting on.

I looked at Max. "Is this about you? Are you worried that her coming out reflects on you? Like you turned her or something?" He didn't answer right away, but his expression gave him away. He kicked at some rocks on the ground.

"Are you? Is that what you think?" Riley asked, the idea landing on her for the first time.

"No. It's not that at all," Max said. I looked right at him, willing him to be honest if he wasn't already. "Really, it's not about my ego. I just don't know what will happen between you and Gracie if she knows. She's not the deepest person I've ever met."

Riley nodded. "Nice. Tell us how you really feel."

"I'm not saying she's not a cool person. I just don't think you can know how she'll take it. So there's risk."

Riley nodded and started gathering up our unused supplies. It had gotten hot again and the fact that I hadn't eaten breakfast was beginning to catch up with me. She was about to answer Max when a whole group showed up, talking loudly and laughing at a joke we didn't hear. Riley clammed right up and picked up a big shovel.

Austin was leading the group, recounting something about last night. "We seriously partied," he was saying. More stories about Talya, I figured.

But Rachel and Kellan were all over his story. "You're such a liar. There's no way Jamie partied with a student. She'd get, like, fired for that," Kellan said.

Austin made a crossing sign over his chest. "Hand to god, she and I smoked out. She had one of those little one-hit-wonder pipes and a pocket full of weed."

"I don't believe you," Rachel said, giving him a playful punch. The sight of Austin had zero effect on me now, other than a slightly nauseating feeling in my gut. But I'd smelled the pot smell on Jamie myself, so even though I knew better than to believe a word he said, I knew it wasn't impossible.

They kept walking down the trail, and Riley and Max followed a couple paces behind them. We were all baking in the heat and dying to get down the hill into the shade. We didn't have an afternoon project, so once we had lunch, we could start packing up for the drive back home. I got a chill just thinking about going home, sleeping in my own bed, and seeing my family. I picked up a bucket of tools and started to follow the group. Austin hung back and fell in step with me.

"Looking for a new audience for your tall tales?" I asked. I didn't slow my pace down. My head ached and I was hot. I looked behind and saw Jamie and Bryce loading the rest of the gear into the truck. I wondered if Jamie had heard Austin talking about her.

He kept up with my pace and ran a couple feet ahead of me to walk backward, watching me instead of his feet. I gestured for him to look behind himself when he almost ran into a tree. He nimbly avoided it just in time, still keeping his eyes on me. "Nah, I'm looking for you."

I rolled my eyes. "Austin, enough, okay?"

He pretended to take a dagger to the heart. "You're killing me. I thought maybe you'd given it some time to wash over you."

"What?"

"Me. What I said last night. I don't want another party. I want you."

I picked up my pace, trying to catch up to the others, but with the bucket of tools, I couldn't walk as fast as I wanted to. I tried to ignore Austin but he wouldn't let me pass. Finally, I put on the brakes. "Stop. Okay? Why does everything you say have to come out like a bad pickup line? Can't you just be honest, like a normal person?"

A ground squirrel darted down a tree and across the path in front of me, making me jump.

"I am being honest."

"You're telling me what you think I want to hear. But, Austin, you're not getting it. I don't want to hear that. I really don't."

He kept walking backward but slowed his pace. He looked at the sky like he was piecing all my new information together. I could tell he was used to using his charms to get his way and it confused him when they weren't working. "Okay," he said finally.

"Okay, great."

I swung the bucket to give myself some forward momentum and moved as quickly as I could to force him to pick up the pace, too. Austin reached over and grabbed the bucket out of my hands. "At least let me take this." I wasn't going to argue.

Riley, Jaden, Max, and Gracie were walking together on the trail and I caught up to them just when I heard

Austin say, loudly, "Whatever, Callie. It's cool. I just don't know why you didn't say you were a lesbian from the beginning. It would have saved me a lot of time and energy."

Riley looked at me, bright red. Even though she knew he wasn't talking about her, Austin's timing couldn't have been worse. "Austin, give it a rest," I told him, shooting him a warning look.

He shrugged. "It's no biggie, Callie. If you're into that, just be honest about it."

I looked at Max, who was looking at Riley, who was looking at the ground.

Finally, Gracie broke the tension by laughing out loud. "Austin, shut the hell up. Callie's not into girls. She's just not into you."

"Ooh," Jaden said. "You just got schooled."

"I don't think so. Callie acts like she doesn't feel it, but she'll come around to me. I've just gotta be patient."

I hadn't noticed Talya sitting a few yards away on a rock, taking in the whole scene. I met her eyes, trying to communicate that there was no truth to what Austin was saying. There wasn't and never would be anything between us. She and I hadn't spoken since last night and I knew she was still angry that I'd told her Austin was bad news. This didn't help.

"We're heading down, you wanna come?" I asked her. She shook her head.

"I'm good," she said.

Austin followed my gaze and saw Talya sitting there. He hesitated, then looked at me for guidance. "Here's your chance not to be a jerk," I said quietly to him. He still didn't make a move, but I knew he understood that I was right. The rest of us turned and made our way down the trail, leaving Austin and Talya behind.

Chapter 22

"*I decided I'm gonna do it.* I'm gonna tell her," Riley said to me and Max after we'd changed out of our grubby work clothes and headed to the picnic benches to chill before lunch. Max looked at me, unsure how to counsel her.

I looked around to see if we had an audience, but everyone was still back at the tents or the showers and Bryce and Jamie were strangely out of sight. Riley dealt a hand of cards to each of us and kept talking like she'd prepared a speech and didn't need our feedback. "Look, we've been friends, like, forever. We've gone through a lot. I think she can handle it. Knowing."

Max picked up his hand of cards and kept his head

down. He'd already given his opinion and maybe he didn't want to get into it again.

"I think it's a good idea. I think you should tell her. She's your best friend, you owe her that," I said. "I mean, if it were me, I'd want to know."

Riley smiled. "I would, too. But for different reasons." She picked up her cards and studied them. I didn't even know what game we were playing. Max was looking intently at his own hand, mainly so he could avoid making eye contact with Riley.

"What's up, Max? Why the cone of silence?" I said.

A gray bird swooped down from a tree branch overhead and landed on the picnic table. It hopped along, pecking occasionally but not finding much of anything to eat. Either we'd done a pretty good job of cleaning up after breakfast or another animal or bird had gotten there first. "No luck, eh, buddy?" Max said. The bird pecked at the wood one more time, then flew off.

"Yeah, Max, what's up? Are you that against me telling her?"

Max shrugged. The shrug of a thousand unspoken thoughts.

"What? Speak," Riley said.

Max put down his cards. The bird flew back to our table and pecked at the cards before Max shooed it away. "Paper's not food, bird." But he still didn't answer Riley.

"So, how are you gonna tell her? Are you just gonna blurt it out or lay some groundwork or what?" I asked.

Max stood up. "Okay, look, I don't think it's a good idea to tell her. I mean, she's not gay. We know that. So I don't see her suddenly changing into a different person. If anything, it'll be totally awkward between the two of you and you'll lose your best friend. There's no upside for you, Riley. Zero."

"Why are you so down on this?" I asked. This wasn't the mellow guy who I'd spent two days getting to know. He was wringing his hands and getting seriously worked up. "I mean, this can't be easy for Riley, carrying this around. Even if Gracie doesn't feel the same way, she'll understand. Riley's her best friend."

Jamie came out with a tray of fruit but I caught her eye and shook my head. Not the time. She quietly put the tray down on a different table and moved silently back to the food prep area. But she kept an eye on us from where she worked.

Max picked up a rock and hurled it at a tree. It rebounded and practically hit me in the head. He looked shocked at the almost accident. I put a hand on his shoulder. He looked at me and took a deep breath, prepping himself for something. Finally, he unleashed it all. "I know how it feels to tell a person you love them and have them stare at you and say nothing, okay? It doesn't feel good."

Riley looked at the ground, so I couldn't read her expression. When she looked up, she was on the verge of tears. I guess she was thinking about how it would feel if she opened up to Gracie and got nothing in return. Turns out I was wrong. Again. "You mean me?" she asked.

Max nodded, the anguish streaking his face. He stuffed his hands in his pockets and walked a few paces away. I couldn't say a thing. Of anyone, I was probably the worst person to ask about love. Riley got up and walked over to him. "I'm so sorry. I never really knew it was this hard for you."

"'Cause I didn't tell you. How would you have felt if you knew what you did to me?"

"I would have felt awful. But I wish you'd told me. I really do."

Max nodded. He said nothing, pacing back and forth, while Riley and I watched and let him sort it all out. I knew I should just give him space, but it was hard not to say anything. Finally, he turned and nodded. "You should tell Gracie," he said. "And I hope you get what you want."

Chapter 23

While Jamie was getting the food out to make lunch, I decided to go back to our bunk for some sunscreen. My skin was fried and even though I knew it was practically useless to put sunscreen on top of a burn, I had to do something. Before I left, I went over to where she was, feeling strange about last night. I wondered if she really had been high and if she even remembered running into us.

"Hey, Jamie, can I help with anything?" I asked.

"Nah, I'm good. Thanks, Callie."

I lingered, expecting to hear a vintage Jamie soliloquy about nature or our duty to mother earth. She was busy rifling through the cooler for something and didn't seem that interested in a conversation, which felt odd. But I didn't push. She turned her back and started grabbing from a pile of firewood and collecting pine needles. It would have been much easier if I'd helped her so I waited, expecting her to relent and give me a job, but she kept working as if I wasn't there. So after another minute, I went back to my bunk.

When I opened the door, the first thing I saw was Talya's pile of clothes, which had grown to the size of a mini mountain on her bed. What I didn't see immediately was Talya on the other side of the mess. Not until she spoke. "Close the door."

"Oh, hey. I didn't know you were here. What's with the Tasmanian devil action?"

She sat up. "Huh?"

"You know, the cartoon?" She looked at me blankly. "Whatever. Not important." I could tell she'd been crying but I decided to take my cues from her. If she wanted to talk about it, great. If not, I'd just get my sunscreen and go. I started rifling through my bag. Of course the sunscreen had fallen to the very bottom. My packing and unpacking process was the polar opposite of what was going on over on Talya's bed. I kept everything in my bag at all times and just ransacked my way through when I needed something. The result was a complete disaster of rumpled clothes and no sense of order at this point, but at least everything was still in the bag. It would make packing up take about three minutes. Couldn't say the same for Talya.

While I was rummaging through, I came across Jude's Padres baseball hat. He must've packed it hoping I'd find it later. I picked it up and held it to my chest, suddenly missing him more than I had this entire weekend. I had to adjust the strap at the back, but then it fit perfectly. If only I'd found it yesterday, I could have saved myself a skin cancer lecture from Lena when I got home.

My sunscreen stick was nowhere to be found, so I continued shuffling the clothes around in my bag, covering for the otherwise uncomfortable silence. "You were right," Talya said. "About Austin."

I turned to look at her. "Are you okay?"

"I will be," she sighed. "I don't know why I didn't see it. He was never gonna be serious about me."

"You didn't want to see it. Don'tcha think we all do that?"

"It's pretty stupid. I actually believed what he said."

"He's an easy guy to believe. He's good at getting what he wants. And he's charming." Though I'd gotten over his charms. I saw exactly where they would lead and Talya was proof that it was nowhere good. I felt bad for her.

"I'm really sorry I told him about Brandon. I never should have said anything. I kind of felt like it was my information to share since it was about me, too, but I know it was worse for you," she said.

189

I nodded. "Thanks for saying that."

"Can we, like, put it behind us?"

"Sure," I said. We would be getting back on the bus after lunch, and the whole past forty-eight hours was starting to feel like one big hurdle, but I could see my way to the other side. By Monday we'd be back at school, and I couldn't tell if we'd just push all this under the rug or if it would linger.

Talya rolled over on her bed, pushing half the clothes onto the floor. I picked up a towel and started rolling it up, wanting to help her move on. Maybe it would just come in the form of housekeeping. Talya grabbed a shirt and followed my lead, rolling it up. "Easier to pack this way, right?" I said. That was a Stef trick—rolling everything up and packing end to end so I could see everything at once. My bag looked great when I'd first left home but if she could see it now, she'd be horrified.

"Am I just the biggest loser or what?" she asked.

I sat on the edge of her bed. "Not at all."

"Why do I have such bad luck with guys?"

"Maybe you're just picking the wrong ones," I said. "God, that sounds so cliché." Talya sat up and straightened her hair, tying it up in a ponytail. She shook her head, like she was trying to shake off the bad karma.

"Maybe 'cause it's true," she said. She pushed the rest of her clothes to the side and stood up. "For one thing, I have to quit picking guys who are into you."

"Talya, I swear—"

"No, I know. I was kidding," she said. "Sort of." She laughed.

I adjusted my baseball cap, feeling something weird in the brim. I looked and saw that Jude had left me a note folded up in the band. "Have fun, but not too much. Love you, J."

"I'm so glad we're heading home today. I love this mountain air, but I'll never take a smoggy city day for granted again," I said. "I'm gonna go see if Jamie's done getting lunch ready. You coming?"

"In a minute. I just want to be by myself for a bit." I studied her face to make sure she was okay. "Really. I'm not gonna burn the place down. I'm just not ready to . . . see everyone."

"Okay. Understood."

I started to go, but she called me back. "Callie? I just want you to know I appreciate that you tried to help me. I really hope we can be friends." She started packing up her bags without waiting for me to respond, maybe because she didn't want to hear my answer.

"Of course we can," I told her. "We're already friends." I saw her smile.

It had gotten hot again, but this time I didn't feel myself plotting ways to avoid the heat. I walked back to the benches, admiring the way the light pitched through the tree branches at sharp angles that looked like prism beams. It felt good to be outside, but I couldn't help thinking that part of why I suddenly felt so free and relieved was because I would be heading home soon.

The scent of barbecued burgers wafted through the air. "Thank god, we won't have to stare down another plate of warm turkey and cheese," Riley said, walking up behind me. "I think I might puke."

"Hey. Did you talk to her?" Riley nodded. "So?"

She shook her head. She was carrying a pad of paper and some colored pencils.

"You don't want to talk about it, that's cool," I said.

"There's nothing to talk about. I told Gracie. She freaked. Said she needs some time away from me. For a while. I don't even know what that means." She forced a smile through gritted teeth.

"It probably just means she needs to process it. She'll come around."

"Crazy thing is, she said she kind of already knew. How weird is that? For the longest time, I didn't even know."

I didn't know what to say. My advice about spilling it all, going with your gut, might have led Riley to sabotage her relationship with her best friend. Maybe you can't trust your instincts all the time. "I didn't know you were an artist," I said.

She opened her sketch pad and flipped through some pages, all colored sketches of different plant species we'd seen on this trip. I hadn't even seen her with her sketch-pad before now but she'd obviously been hard at work on it.

"Yeah, just a hobby."

"You're good at it."

Riley shrugged. She started walking toward camp. "I'm hungry. Isn't that strange? I'm a wreck but my body still insists on food."

"It's gonna be okay," I called after her.

"Yeah," she said. "I think so, too."

Chapter 24

The bus sped down the mountain roads and I watched the trees recede in the distance while the gray of highways took over the landscape. Inside the bus, the air conditioner kept us at a cool sixty-eight degrees and the plush seats felt luxurious compared with our spare bunks. Gone was the nervous anticipation and energy we'd had on the ride up, the anxiety that went with being away from home and spending time with people we maybe didn't know. Everyone was quieter, but for differing reasons.

There was more space to spread out now because a bunch of the seats on the way up had been taken up by food and gear. Jamie had brought up a whole new set of kitchen supplies that would stay at camp for the summer. Plus the bags of food she'd brought up were gone and the coolers empty, so they got thrown under the bus with our bags. The result was that a lot of us had two seats to ourselves, and I didn't really mind not having company.

I felt calmer now, knowing I'd gotten through the challenge of integrating myself into yet another new group of kids. I'd succeeded at building and cleaning and hauling, so I could see my way clear to a GPA that didn't threaten to hold me back a year in school. And I was going home, which just felt good. Riley and Gracie started out the ride sitting a few seats away from each other, sitting right in front of me . . . leaning over the front of my seat.

She nodded. "Yeah. I can't believe I actually did it. I feel . . . relieved. And also a little stuck. Now I'm in this, whatever it means, however long it takes to get ourselves back to a place where we can be friends."

I understood exactly what she meant. There's something great about knowing that wherever the path leads, you're committed to it. Even if it doesn't take you where you expect it to go, you're moving in a direction and making some kind of progress. "So you're not bummed you told her?" I asked.

"No. I think it's good. I mean, in a perfect world, she would have said she feels the same way and maybe someday . . ." She shook her head. "Am I just making stuff up? Or is it possible?"

"I don't know. Maybe with Gracie. Maybe with someone else. But at least you're out now. That has to feel good."

"It's gonna be weird going back to school next week. Word has a way of getting out. People are gonna know and they're gonna talk." She took a deep breath, preparing herself.

"For a minute. Then they're going to move on to the next drama and you'll be able to be yourself. That's a good thing."

Riley looked down by her feet and grabbed something. She sat up and flipped open her sketchbook. I saw she'd drawn a picture of me and Max. Even though I'd had my hair up in a ponytail all weekend long, she'd drawn it down and flowing like a goddess or mermaid or something. Max looked happy, the side of him I'd seen when we first met, before all the talk about Riley coming out. Something about the picture captured what I felt about Max, that he and I shared a bond neither of us could really describe, like we'd known each other much longer than this weekend. Only where our bodies should've been, she'd drawn tree trunks and roots extending down into the ground. We each had branches for arms and the leaves on our outstretched branches were one and the same. "You guys helped me through this," she said. "Thanks."

I looked at the sketch. "It's amazing. You're really talented." She smiled. "I don't think I look like that most of the time, or even any of the time, necessarily. But it's how I wish I could be."

"That's what's so great about art." She flipped through the book, then hesitated before showing me another set of pencil sketches she'd done of Gracie. She looked beautiful in those pictures. Riley had spent a lot of time thinking about her, even dreaming about her. She looked at them herself for a minute, then snapped the book shut. "It's stupid. It's like I've created this whole fantasy world of us together."

"You still have a lot of that. As a friend."

"I know. And I can handle just being friends and not having it go further. I just hope she can." I looked a few rows up at where Gracie was sitting, her head down in a copy of *People* magazine.

Riley grabbed a sweatshirt, crumpled it into a ball, and leaned it against the window. A nap sounded really good to me, too, right now. I had slept pretty well the past two nights, but something about the altitude mixed with the physical work and my bumpy emotions left me exhausted now. I thought about doing the same as Riley. I'd left my sweatshirts in my duffel and only had a book and a water bottle in my daypack. Not exactly the makings of a comfortable pillow.

I hadn't talked to Austin since leaving him and Talya on the trail earlier. He'd been keeping his head down, and during lunch, took his burger back to his bunk and ate while he packed. But now he was back, slipping into the seat next to me. But instead of starting in with one of his one-liners, he just looked straight ahead like he didn't notice I was there.

"Hey," I said after a minute.

He looked at me, his head tilted to the side like he was thinking about what to say. Or what not to say. I didn't really want to get into a whole discussion so I let it be. Maybe we could just sit on the bus and say nothing. I leaned my head back and closed my eyes.

"So, you remember how you asked me to be honest?"

I opened my eyes. "Yeah."

"So all this . . . you know . . . how I've been this weekend? It's kind of 'cause I feel like it's my last chance." He was looking at me like I would know what he meant. But I didn't.

"Last chance for what?"

He sat back in his chair and looked at the ceiling of the bus. It had a pattern of squiggly lines that looked like lightning on a light blue background. It reminded me of Jamie's words: "Always look up." I guess they didn't apply just out in nature. "I'm flunking out of school," he said finally, looking me in the eye.

His pale green eyes no longer had the power to warm me from the inside out, but there was no denying that he was nice to look at. I just didn't know if I could believe him.

"Seriously? This isn't another attempt to get my attention?"

He made a cross over his heart. "Trust me, I wish I was joking about this one."

"So what does that mean?" I asked.

He looked around at the kids on the bus, some sleeping, some reading, others grouped together in conversation. A mellow scene but one you'd miss if you were being booted out of school. "I've missed a lot of school, just screwing around. Ditching 'cause I was bored. My GPA isn't exactly stellar. It was stupid, and if I had it to do over again . . . well, I don't know if I'd do it that differently. I start off with good intentions about studying, and then I just . . . lose focus." He looked seriously bummed. It was so different from the way I went about things, thinking so hard about everyone and everything all the time.

"Hey, we all have our reasons for being here. Not all of us are trying to get early admission to Yale. My GPA isn't so hot, trust me." I wondered if he already knew that. "But won't this weekend help? I mean, I'm getting two units of independent study and if you factor in a 4.0 on those with everything else, can't that give you enough to get by?"

He shrugged. "Prolly not. So, um, this weekend, I was just trying to find my way. I guess I don't really know how to do that."

"Why are you telling me this?" I asked.

"I just wanted you to understand. Where I'm coming from. That I'm more than just a jerk." Then he realized how that sounded and smiled a little.

I laughed. "How much more?"

He picked up the book I'd been reading and looked at the cover. "This any good?"

I shrugged. "Each time I pick it up I read about a page, and the next time I can't remember what happened, so I read the same page again."

"Yup. Been there," he said. He flipped through. Then he turned to the first page, cracked the spine open and started reading.

I looked up when I saw Gracie coming down the aisle. She smiled at me and I figured she was coming to talk, but she stopped at the seat one ahead of mine and slid in next to Riley, who was still asleep by the window. Gracie watched her for a minute, then tapped her on the shoulder. Riley opened one eye and a smile spread across her face. I leaned back toward Austin and read over his shoulder, feeling the cool blast of the AC from overhead and seeing words I'd read at least a couple times before.

Chapter 25

The bus turned a corner and I glimpsed the park a block ahead. Before we turned into the driveway, I could already see a mass of people gathered in the parking lot. I tried to pick out faces in the crowd but we were still too far away.

Everything looked the same as I remembered it, but somehow different. I knew I'd only been gone for forty-eight hours but I'd covered a lot of ground, some of it on foot and some of it in other ways. I just felt like I was different than I would've been if I had stayed at home all weekend long. I'd have to remember to thank Lena for insisting I take this trip, even if my attitude beforehand hadn't been stellar.

I got my chance as soon as the bus turned off its engine. Lena was right up in front of the crowd, waving, with Stef by her side, telling her what I was sure was "You're just waving at a bus. Callie may not even be able to see you." Then she started waving, too.

All of us were moving in slow motion when the bus driver opened the door. It was partly the inevitable good-byes, which we weren't looking forward to, and another very real issue: our arms, legs, backs, and all other moving parts were so sore from lugging equipment, hiking hills, and building stairs and bridges that it hurt to stand. Austin had fallen asleep with his head on the armrest between us but he popped his head up when the door opened and ran a hand through his hair, rumpling it in a perfectly imperfect way. I smiled.

"What?" he asked, still sleepy.

"Nothing. You happy to be back?" He looked out the window, maybe searching for his parents in the group.

"Okay, who are these happy ladies in the front here? They look like they haven't seen their kids in a year. Get a life, why don'tcha?" Even without looking, I knew he was talking about Stef and Lena.

"Those are my foster moms."

"Oh. Ouch."

"Nah, it's cool. That's just how they are."

We gathered our stuff and made our way off the bus.

I practically fell on top of Lena who was hugging the side of the bus like she was scared she might miss me if she took a step back. "Lena!" I said. She wrapped me up in a bear hug. Stef was next.

We moved away from the bus and made room for everyone else to get off, and they walked me over to where Brandon was waiting on the grass. I looked around for the rest of my family, but I didn't see them.

"Oh, we missed you! I know it was only two days, but still."

"You have to forgive Mama, she just loves you."

I hugged them both again then looked up at Brandon, who was standing with two guys I didn't know. Brandon looked relieved to see me, then annoyed. I knew why. I'd blown him off, or we'd blown each other off, on the road that night. We needed to sort that out, but not here in front of Lena and Stef. "Callie, these are a couple of the guys from work, Randy and Charles," Stef said.

They both extended their hands. "Nice to meet you. This one's trouble, you know that, right?" Randy said, pointing to Stef. "In fact, I could tell you some stories about her that would—"

"Okay, okay, let's move it along, boys," Stef said, herding them away.

Brandon grabbed my elbow and steered me away. "Hey, Callie and I'll go find her bags, ok? You guys can stay and talk or whatever." We left them behind and headed to where the bags were being thrown out of the luggage compartment beneath the bus. I was glad I hadn't packed anything fragile.

"So, what happened to you last night?" Brandon asked the second we were alone.

"Brandon, I wanted to meet you. I wasn't even sure if you'd come."

"Well, I came, okay? And waited. You scared the crap out of me. I thought you got abducted or something."

"I know, I'm sorry—"

"No, actually, I'm glad. It was dicey out there. I waited about an hour but seriously, in the time I was out there I didn't see anyone, not a car, nothing. So then I figured you came to your senses and decided not to risk getting booted off the trip by sneaking out."

For about a second, I considered telling him about my night, about how I snuck out and worried about getting run over by a semi. And about how Max had come after me and saved my butt. Then I decided to let him think I'd made the right decision, let him think the better of me. "Yeah, I'm sorry I scared you. I just . . . you know, wanted to stay on the straight and narrow."

"Smart. Good idea," he said, looking me over. I wondered if he could tell I was lying.

"What?" I asked.

"Nothing."

Everyone was hugging good-bye and getting into their

respective cars. I said good-bye to Gracie and Riley, who were going home with Gracie's parents. They seemed a little uneasy with each other but I sensed it was only temporary. I wondered if Gracie's parents would notice. Jaden found his uncle in the crowd and was leaving in a hurry because he had lacrosse practice, and Max gave me a quick kiss on the cheek with a promise he'd text after practice. I was a little sad to leave all of them, but it didn't feel like I was losing these new friends. We'd already made plans for a reunion without hiking or hauling rocks. I saw Austin standing by himself watching everyone else. I wondered if his parents hadn't showed. "Hang on just a sec," I said to Brandon, and walked over.

"You need a ride someplace? We've got two cars, tons of room."

"Thanks, but nah. My parents are here."

"Oh, yeah?" I looked around, curious about what his parents looked like. I didn't see anyone who seemed to obviously belong to Austin.

He pointed to a couple standing talking to Bryce. His dad had on khaki pants and a yellow button-up shirt with a white cotton sweater tied around his shoulders. He was wearing a pair of loafers and I could see from here that he didn't have on socks. Austin's mom stood next to him with her arms crossed. Her hair was clipped up in a high ponytail and she wore yoga pants with a tight workout jacket, and I had the feeling she actually had come from a Pilates class or something. Bryce was doing most of the talking and they were nodding.

"The parents didn't waste any time before dropping the news. Apparently my school isn't gonna accept this weekend for outside credit after all. My folks are trying to see if Bryce can maybe do something, but . . . it's not looking good."

"Why aren't they giving you credit?"

He shrugged. But I got the sense he knew the reason. Austin looked at his shoes, then shook his head. "You remember the whole thing when I told people I smoked out with Jamie? Bryce filed a report. He said he had to, or he'd be the one fired."

It made sense now, why I hadn't seen much of Jamie today. "So, you got her fired?"

Austin looked like he felt really awful about it. "I don't know. It's between her and Bryce, but needless to say, it's not helping me get my credit for the project."

"Is there anything you can do?"

He didn't have a chance to respond. His parents called him over to where they were still standing with Bryce. He jogged over to them, his head hanging low. There was more to him than I'd gotten to know this weekend, and I couldn't decide if I was intrigued or still a little distrusting of him.

I looked back at Brandon and saw him talking to Talya. Suddenly, they both looked at me and laughed, making me wonder what they were saying. Seeing them together dredged up old feelings, and that surprised me.

"Hey, you, are you a total hippie chick now?" Mariana squealed, running over to hug me. Jesus and Jude were right behind her.

"If building two bridges and knowing a few constellations qualifies me as a hippie chick, then yeah," I said. I was kind of proud of my new skills.

"Watch out, she'll be building a yurt in the backyard," Jesus said. He checked his phone, which kept beeping with text messages. His thumbs started tapping away in response.

"Hey, I'm not the one who even knows what a yurt is," I said.

Jesus slapped me a high five and Jude grabbed me around the waist in a huge bear hug. "You didn't miss me, Jude. Quit pretending. You probably hogged my share of Lena's brownies while I was gone."

"No comment," he said. He stared at his hat, which I was still wearing. "Did you find my note?"

"I did. It was awesome. Thanks." He grinned and reached up and plucked the hat off my head.

"Don't get any ideas. It was a loan," he said, putting the hat on. Then he ran over to get Lena and Stef, who were still talking to her cop friends.

Brandon carried my bags to the car, with Jesus and Mariana trailing behind, talking about some party they'd gone to the night before. "Man, it was epic. Callie, you should have heard the band. They had two drummers and they did this thing . . ."

I nodded, not really hearing what he was saying. My head was still caught in the weekend and I looked around one last time at everyone piling into cars and heading home. Brandon popped the trunk and loaded my stuff. Talya's parents were parked a couple spots over, but before she left, she came over to say good-bye.

"Hey. I'll see you at school tomorrow, 'k?" she said.

I reached to give her a hug and saw Austin jogging over to say good-bye. I felt her tense up, but she plastered on a big smile. I didn't introduce Brandon. Who knew what Austin was liable to say to him? "So? Any luck getting things straightened out?" I asked Austin.

"Nah. I'm getting booted for sure. The pot situation kind of pushed the whole thing over." Brandon shot me a look: *What's the deal with this guy?* I returned the look: *I'll tell you all about it later.*

"What are you guys talking about?" Talya asked.

"I'm switching schools. Probably going public. You guys go to Anchor Beach, right? Is it decent?"

A lump sank from my throat to the pit of my stomach. What was he saying? "Um, sure," I said. "Why?"

"I might be seeing you there. I'm in the district, so it's a natural. I can start tomorrow." He shrugged. "I don't know. We'll see. My folks are gonna have to work it all out."

Talya was staring at him, mouth agape. I didn't know what to say. Austin's parents called him and waved him back. "Gotta go," he said, trotting away like he hadn't just leveled us with his news.

I looked at Talya. She looked at me, both of us waiting for the other one to say something. There was nothing to say. Which made us both crack up.

Epilogue

There's something strange about the clock above the door. Every time the second hand sweeps past the fat black number ten and makes its way to the eleven, the clock hums like it's digesting a swarm of bees. Then back to silence. Looking around the room, I expect everyone in the class to have the same interrupted train of thought I have when the humming kicks in every fifty-five seconds, but no one else seems to be bothered. They're just deep in thought. Or devoid of thought. Lucky either way.

I've never been a clock-watcher. And after the past weekend, I have a little better appreciation for the ability to unplug and let things unfold however they do, without trying to control them too much.

213

But it's almost impossible not to think about how things might unfold if Austin ends up coming to Anchor Beach. I looked for him this morning before the bell, but I didn't see any sign of him. I know him well enough to assume that he'll find a way to make his presence obvious. But it's still early. If he's here, we'll find each other at lunch or at break or at the lockers between classes. I mean, it's inevitable, right? There's going to be drama, or at the very least, it's just going to be damned uncomfortable. Because that's how we left things, not really knowing where any of us stood.